California Awakening

by

Mark Sahl

Eduardo Vega, Illustrator

© Copyright 2020, California Awakening, **Mark Sahl**

All rights reserved. No part of this book may be reproduced, distributed, or transmitted in any form or by any means, including photocopying, recording, or other electronic or mechanical methods, without the prior written permission of the publisher.

ISBN: 979-8-89397-873-5

Edition: First

Published by Booklyn Writers

Table of Contents

Chapter 1

Luke:

"C'mon Mark. Less than a mile to go."

Mark's legs are heavy from the first four miles of their run. The soles of Mark's bare feet alternatively feel the coolness of the softball and soccer fields' grass, followed by the mid-afternoon heat of the black asphalt road bordering the fields on Kwajalein, a small boomerang-shaped island in the South Pacific's Marshall Islands. His T-shirt sticks to his sweaty torso.

Mark:

"I hear ya."

Bicyclists on their way home from work pass them.

Encouraged by Luke's words, Mark finds a final burst of energy, and the 10-year-old best friends run side by side, their breath fast and even. As they round the final turn, the end comes into sight: the jogging club's outdoor cork message board. Luke races ahead.

Luke:

"Last one there's a rotten egg!"

Mark:

"No fair!"

Luke finishes seconds ahead of Mark.

They slow to a walk, circling the board several times to cool down. They stop at the board's tracking chart with one row of squares per member. One filled-in square is one mile run. Luke's and Mark's are halfway filled in, and each of the boys darkens in five more squares using the pencil hanging from the board.

Mark:

"We've both done more than 70 miles."

Luke:

"Not bad."

The boys walk over to their bikes in the long, rusty bike stand next to the board. They unlock and get on them, riding over to the dependents' pool close by. After depositing their bikes in a matching stand, Mark and Luke climb the 10 concrete steps at the pool's entrance and go through the gate of the chain-link fence around the pool. The local hangout is crowded with kids and teenagers, some playfully swimming, others taking turns diving and jumping off the two diving boards at the deep end. Mark and Luke peel off their T-shirts and dive into the refreshing salt water. As Mark swims underwater, he feels his body further cool down. He looks sideways at Luke swimming beside him and then up at the others on the surface.

Captain Stewart:

"Aloha, folks. Good morning. This is Captain Stewart again."

The pilot's deep, reassuring voice startles Mark out of his daydream.

It's just before dawn on June 24, 1976, nearly three weeks after his 15th birthday, and he's a passenger in a 747 winging its way from Honolulu to San Francisco. 30,000 feet over the dark-blue Pacific Ocean, Mark is seated in an economy window seat, and his reclined body is leaning against the plane's fuselage.

All the window shades are down in the darkened cabin. The flight is full of Hawaiians visiting mainland relatives, tourists at the end of their vacations, and salesmen returning from a national sales meeting in Waikiki. Most are asleep, but some are reading or watching the final scene of *Close Encounters of the Third Kind* with Richard Dreyfuss. Farrah Fawcett smiles broadly on the cover of the *People* magazine laying in the empty middle seat next to him, and a pillow and blanket are draped across the empty aisle seat.

As the final movie credits roll, the overhead lights come on.

Captain Stewart:

"We hope you've had a restful night and enjoyed your flight. We'll be touching down in San Francisco in about an hour. The temperature is 55 degrees, and it's foggy. Our stewardesses are doing the last cabin check. Mahalo for flying United."

Mark yawns and stretches his arms and legs.

Sarah, the occupant of the aisle seat, returns from the bathroom. She is 19 and wears an oversized dark-green

University of Hawaii sweatshirt and faded bell-bottom jeans. Her feet are bare, and her shoulder-length sun-bleached hair is pulled back in a loose ponytail. Sarah lifts the blanket and pillow off her seat as she sits back down.

Sarah:

"Hey."

Mark:

"Hey."

Sarah:

"You were out of it there for a while."

Mark:

"Yeah, thinking back. My body clock is off because of the time change."

Sarah:

"Oh, where are you coming from?"

Mark:

"The Marshall Islands, where I live with my family."

Sarah:

"Where are the Marshalls?"

Mark:

"Southwest of Hawaii. We're on Kwajalein Atoll."

Sarah:

"Interesting. Why is your family living there?"

Mark:

"My dad is a computer systems analyst working on the U.S.'s long-range defense missile system."

Sarah:

"When did you move there?"

Mark:

"Seven years ago from Philadelphia. I see you're wearing a U of H sweatshirt. You go there?"

Sarah:

"Yeah, I just finished my second year of nursing in Hono."

Mark:

"Cool."

Sarah:

"Finals were intense. Felt like I was living in the library for the last few weeks."

Mark:

"How did you do?"

Sarah:

"Pretty well. Definitely ready for a break."

Mark:

"Where you from?"

Sarah:

"San Francisco. I'm spending the summer there with my folks and younger sister, Beth."

Mark:

"Must have been a great place to grow up."

Sarah:

"I can't wait to see them."

Mark:

"What are your plans for the summer?"

Sarah:

"I'm waitressing at Fisherman's Grotto on Fisherman's Wharf. It's actually going to be my second summer there. Really can use the money for college."

Mark:

"Yeah, I'm saving for school too, with my bar mitzvah money and being a lifeguard."

Sarah:

"Also looking forward to hanging out with my high school friends. What about you?"

Mark:

"This is my first trip on my own."

Sarah:

"You staying in San Francisco?"

Mark:

"I'm going to Santa Cruz to spend about a week with my friend Luke and his family.''

Sarah:

"Sounds like fun."

Mark:

"Yeah. Luke and his mom are picking me up. We met on Kwaj in elementary school, but his family moved back to California when we were in junior high. We've written some, but this'll be the first time we've seen each other since then."

Sarah:

"I think you'll like it. I've spent time at the beach and boardwalk there."

Mark:

"I'm unsure how things will go."

Sarah:

"You just need to get to know each other again."

Mark:

"Thanks, Sarah. Your mom and dad picking you up at the airport?"

Sarah:

"Yes, Beth too. I talked with mom last night. Knowing them, they'll do something cheesy."

Mark:

"I don't even know how Luke looks now. I've changed. But I'll recognize his mom."

A stewardess stops at their row:

"You need to put up your seats and secure your seat belts and tray tables."

Smiling at the stewardess, they get ready for landing. The other passengers also put away their belongings under seats and in overhead bins.

Sarah picks up the *People* and starts reading about Farrah's new poster and TV show, *Charlie's Angels*. Mark lifts the window blind and looks out. The plane has descended to a few thousand feet, the sun is peeking over the horizon and through the clouds, and the coastline is in view. Fog covers downtown San Francisco, with the tip of the pyramid-shaped Transamerica building poking out above the blanket. Mark can make out white caps on the waves below.

Sarah:

"Your legs are shaking."

Mark:

"Nervous energy. I'm excited about seeing Luke. Also kind of nervous about meeting his friends. Luke wrote he has a girlfriend, Stephanie. They've been going out for a year."

Sarah:

"I hope it's a great trip for you."

Mark:

"I hope so, and that you have a good summer."

Sarah:

"I appreciate it. Work, family and friends will take up my time. Beth always wants to be with me, so I have her tag along sometimes with me and my friends."

Mark:

"Yeah, I do the same with my sister Lisa. She's eight years younger than me."

Mark looks outside again and sees the plane's about to touch down.

A 7-year-old boy sitting behind him shakes his mom's shoulder:

"Look, Mom, there's the runway!"

"Yes, honey, we're going to land."

The plane's wheels hit the ground and bounce two times, and Captain Stewart taxis the plane to its gate.

Mark and Sarah unbuckle their seat belts, retrieve their backpacks and wait for the plane to empty.

Mark:

"Thanks again, Sarah, for letting me bend your ear."

Sarah:

"No problem. I enjoyed talking with you. I never knew about Kwaj. Do you like it?"

Mark:

"Yeah. But it's really hot, as we're just north of the equator. There are a few thousand Americans there. Mainly civilians working for defense companies. It's a close-knit community. We do a lot of things together. Sports like softball and inner tube water polo, and other community activities, like an annual four-day carnival. I'm Jewish and there are only a few Jewish families on Kwaj, and the rabbi only flies in every few months. So we take turns leading the Friday night services."

Sarah:

"Sounds nice."

Mark:

"I also swim every morning before school with my team. Our coach, Denny, pushes us but also makes the practices fun. He's a scuba diver for work and helps retrieve the missiles from the lagoon after each mission."

Mark and Sarah finally make their way to the front exit.

Sarah:

"Take care, Mark. Nice meeting you."

Mark:

"Same to you, Sarah. Don't work too hard."

Sarah laughs:

"Don't worry. I'll have some fun too. Bye."

Sarah enters the airport concourse first. She spots her family, holding up a homemade "Welcome Home, Sarah!"

banner. She breaks into a big smile and rushes up to embrace them all at the same time.

Sarah:

"I knew you guys would do something like this. I love it."

She brushes away tears.

Mark smiles as he watches the family reunion, briefly forgetting about Luke and his mom, who are standing a hundred feet away. Luke spots Mark but is unsure it is him. Luke looks at his mom, who nods yes.

Luke:

"Hey, Mark, we're over here."

Mark spots and waves at Luke, then quickly walks over to them. Luke is significantly taller, his long hair several shades darker than from Kwaj and his jawline squarer. Luke's short Portuguese American mom hasn't changed, with her wide hips, short brown-gray hair, dark skin and a kind smile.

Luke and Mark are uncertain how to greet each other. They start to move in to hug, but hesitate and end up in a long handshake, smiling at each other. Luke's mom smiles softly as she watches. Mark then turns to Luke's mom, and she pulls him into a warm hug and then holds him at arm's length to inspect him.

Mark:

"Hi, Mrs. Bordet."

Luke's mom:

"Welcome, honey. You've grown and slimmed down a lot, and look at your short hair!"

Mark smiles and rubs his head.

Luke's mom:

"We're glad you made it safely. The last couple of weeks Luke's been talking my ear off about your visit."

Luke angrily looks at his mom:

"Mom!"

Luke's mom:

"Okay, I'll stop. C'mon boys, let's get Mark's luggage."

The three walk side by side down the crowded concourse.

Luke:

"You must be beat. Can I take your backpack?"

Mark:

"It's okay. I slept on the plane."

Luke and Mark are uncertain of what else to say, and the three walk quietly. Mark looks at the many stores and kiosks. So different from Kwaj, with one small department store, jokingly named Macy's, and the 10-10 convenience store open from 10 am to 10 pm. Luke's mom watches baggage claim directional signs and directs them down the escalators.

Luke finally comes up with something to mention:

"Mom's been cooking up a storm for you."

Mark:

"Thanks, Mrs. Bordet."

She smiles at Mark.

Luke's mom:

"How many suitcases do you have?"

Mark:

"One."

She locates Mark's baggage carousel number on the electronic assignment board, and they walk to it.

Mark:

"I brought Kwaj photos."

Luke:

"Great. We can look at them later."

They arrive at Mark's carousel and wait for his large Samsonite suitcase. He spots it:

"There it is."

Luke:

"I'll get it."

Luke's mom:

"Okay, let's head to the car."

Luke grabs the suitcase pulley handle, positions its wheels facedown and pulls it behind him.

When they get outside, the sun is bright, having burned off the fog. They cross to the parking garage, take the elevator to the third level to Luke's dad's truck, a well-cared-for, dull-yellow 1970 Chevrolet pickup with one bench seat. Luke brings down the truck's tailgate and puts in the suitcase.

Luke's mom sits in the driver's seat, Mark in the center and Luke on the passenger side.

Luke's mom pays for parking at the garage exit and turns right to U.S. Route 101 south.

Mark:

"How long's the drive back to your house?"

Luke's mom:

"About 90 minutes. It's the tail end of rush hour."

Luke and Mark talk, enjoying the sights. The route takes them through Palo Alto and Stanford University, with its Spanish-style academic buildings, and the surrounding residential neighborhoods filled with craftsman and California colonial homes.

Luke:

"How's Catherine?"

Mark:

"Crazy as ever. We have fun at her house, listening to Queen. How are things with Stephanie?"

Luke:

"Good. I think you'll like her. We spend a fair amount of time together, like at her house, hanging out at the backyard pool with friends. It has a diving board, which you'll like."

Mark:

"Yeah, I've been practicing and am getting pretty good."

Luke:

"You'll have to show me."

Mark looks forward to showing off for Luke.

The truck next passes through Mountain View, with its views of the Santa Cruz Mountains for which it's named, and the town of Los Gatos, devoid of its eponymous wild cougars and bobcats. The last leg of the drive takes them through Sierra Azul Preserve, a large, mountainous wilderness area.

Luke's mom:

"I'm glad your mom and dad suggested you visit. Don and I agreed it would be a good chance for you and Luke to catch up."

Mark:

"I'm glad they let me come."

Luke's mom:

"How are they?"

Mark:

"Good. My mom's doing a lot of volunteer work, and when my dad asks what she's making for dinner and she doesn't feel like cooking, she still says, 'Reservations at the Yuk Club.'"

Luke's mom laughs at Mark's joke about the island's one sit-down restaurant, the Yokwe (meaning "hello" in Marshallese) Yuk Club.

Luke's mom:

"That's Joan alright."

Mark:

"My dad played the lead in KCT's production of *Man of La Mancha* and did a great job. He and I enjoy playing tennis together."

Luke's mom:

"Don and I would see him quite a bit at the Kwaj golf course. I miss its great views of the Pacific. Please give them my regards."

Mark:

"Sure."

When Luke's mom gets off the highway, they enter the family's older middle-class suburban neighborhood of Santa Cruz, with small single-family homes set closely together. The streets are winding and tree-covered. Their house is modest, with a full first floor and a finished attic where Luke's bedroom and bathroom are located.

Luke's mom pulls the truck into the driveway and heads toward the back right of the property, where a detached oversized one-car garage sits.

Luke's mom:

"Luke, can you get the garage door?"

Luke gets out of the truck and lifts the door, his mom backs in the truck, and he gets Mark's suitcase and backpack out of the truck bed.

Mark:

"Let me take one of those."

Luke:

"Here's the backpack."

They walk up the stairs at the back of the house into the kitchen.

Luke:

"We'll take this stuff up to my room."

Luke's mom:

"Then come back down. You boys must be hungry."

The kitchen is large and old-fashioned with yellow-and-white cabinets, the upper ones with glass fronts with glasses, cups and dishes showing through. A large rectangular dining table dominates the room's center.

Luke's mom begins taking prepared food from the refrigerator, heating some up and putting the rest directly on the table.

Luke and Mark head upstairs into Luke's bedroom. As they walk into the room, Mark sees it's large with slanted ceilings and two dormer windows at the front. A closet with sliding doors occupies the whole left wall. A waist-high dresser with a large mirror on top sits just inside the room. Two single beds are positioned perpendicular to each other in the corner opposite the closet.

Mark:

"Nice room."

Luke points to the bed directly across from the closet:

"You'll be sleeping there."

Mark puts his suitcase and backpack on his bed.

Luke:

"Let's go and eat."

Mark:

"Yeah. I'm hungry."

Once back in the kitchen, Mark sees Luke's mom has loaded the table with fried chicken, a fresh fruit salad, avocado slices and the makings for ham-and-cheese sandwiches.

Luke's mom:

"Luke, please get some lettuce from out back."

Luke:

"Sure. C'mon, Mark."

Situated next to the garage, the garden is fairly large, with strawberry and raspberry plants and rows of green beans, tomatoes and lettuce. Luke walks over to a row of lettuce and starts picking leaves from the heads for sandwiches.

Luke:

"The trick is choosing the largest and greenest heads."

Mark:

"You know what you're doing."

Luke:

"I spend time out here with my mom in the early mornings. She's taught me a lot. It keeps down our grocery bills, and everything's fresher."

Mark:

"I don't know anything about gardening. The Kwaj soil doesn't grow stuff like this."

Luke:

"I remember the coral infections we got when we didn't clean our cuts well."

Mark:

"One of mine turned into blood poisoning, and I had to lay on the couch for a couple of days with my leg up."

Once Luke finishes picking the lettuce, they head back in, and Luke washes and brings it back to the table on a plate.

The three prepare their plates and eat. After dinner, Mark and Luke clean up and head back upstairs.

Luke slides open the closet. "Here, I cleared out this end of the closet for your clothes."

Mark puts away his things and then places several photo albums on his bed.

Mark:

"Why don't we look at my Kwaj pictures."

They sit next to each other on Mark's bed with their backs against the wall, and Mark opens the first album.

Mark:

"Here's a black-and-white of you and me playing four square on the street next to George Seitz."

Luke:

"There's Lisa on the sidelines watching us play. She was cute. Remember fifth grade with Mr. Healy?"

Mark:

"He had us sing 'You're a Grand Old Flag' every morning."

Luke:

"During summer school, he helped us build ham radios and learn Morse code."

Mark:

"Here we are in a Mischief Night group shaving cream fight in the empty pool. I remember being covered with the stuff by the end and how it stung my eyes."

Luke, pointing to another photo:

"When was this one taken?"

Mark:

"After you moved. It's me at a swim meet in a 1,000-yard race. I came in second."

Luke:

"Which one is you?"

Mark:

"In this lane. Our team trains every morning before school. I ride from our trailer to the pool in the dark. The water's always cold on that first dive."

Luke:

"Trailer 654. Around the corner from ours."

Mark:

"I remember our sleepovers at your place and how your dad would take us in the mornings to hit balls at the golf course."

Luke:

"We had some great times."

Mark:

"I miss you being there. Here are some from a recent Youth Fellowship trip."

Luke:

"Where did you go?"

Mark:

"Majuro, Pohnpei and Guam. Here's the group on the Kwaj airport bleachers, waiting to start the trip. And one of me and Kate on Majuro."

Luke:

"Your hair is long, and your shirt and her dress have the same blue-and-white floral pattern."

Mark:

"We wore matching clothes for musical performances we did for the Marshallese, with instruments and singing, me off-key a lot of the time."

Luke:

"You look like you're taking a group bath here."

Mark:

"That's right, in bathing suits in the river on Pohnpei. We also took turns jumping from the 30-foot-high river bank."

Luke:

"Looks like you were enjoying yourselves."

Mark:

"We were. That picture reminds me of another time in Majuro when we were taking a group shower under a building overhang while it was pouring. What we didn't know is that rainwater is a lot softer than usual, and you only need half as much soap and shampoo. A lot of us were still lathered up when it stopped raining. We had to search for a freshwater hose to finish the process."

Luke:

"That must have been pretty bad."

Mark:

"Let's say I learned how not to shower in the rain."

Luke:

"What about this nighttime photo in the church?"

Mark:

"Most nights we'd sleep on the church floor with the windows open due to the heat. The windows didn't have screens, so we'd cover ourselves in mosquito repellant, wear long-sleeve T-shirts and pants, and burn green mosquito coils. We'd still wake up covered in bites."

Luke:

"Not pleasant, I bet."

Mark:

"Definitely funny to think back on, but it wasn't so nice at the time."

Luke and Mark spend the next few hours talking as they go through the remaining pictures. They become increasingly more comfortable together, sitting close with their legs touching.

As they look at the last of the photos, Luke's mom comes into the bedroom:

"It's dinnertime. Why don't you guys come on down."

After washing up, the two join Luke's mom and dad and brother, Ricky, at the kitchen table, as his mom is putting dinner on. As Luke and Mark sit down, Luke's dad shakes Mark's hand.

Luke's dad:

"Welcome, Mark."

Mark:

"Thanks, Mr. Bordet. Glad to be here."

Luke's dad is a handsome native Californian in his mid-40s. He sports a blond flattop and a belly from his love of beer.

Luke's dad:

"Mom told me about your ride from the airport."

Mark:

"Yeah, it was nice to see some of central California."

Luke's dad:

"We hope you enjoy your stay. But be warned. I will put you and Luke to work."

Luke:

"Dad, don't scare him off!"

Mark:

"I'm glad to help."

Luke's dad:

"I'll remember that."

As Mark enjoys his first Santa Cruz dinner, it reminds him of dinners with the Bordets on Kwaj.

After dessert, Luke excuses himself and Mark:

"We're going to turn in. Good night, mom and dad."

Luke's mom gives her son a hug.

Luke's mom:

"Night, boys. We're glad to have you, Mark."

Luke's dad:

"Good night."

Luke and Mark go into the bedroom, now dark except for streetlamp light streaming in the windows. Luke turns on the nightstand lamp between the beds and takes out blue gym shorts and a gray T-shirt from the top dresser drawer.

He thinks about getting changed in the room with Mark but, feeling modest, opts to change in the bathroom when he brushes his teeth.

While Luke's gone, Mark changes, quickly deposits his dirty clothes on the closet floor and climbs into bed, where he lies on his back, takes a deep breath and relaxes as Luke returns to the bedroom.

Mark and Luke smile at each other as Luke gets into bed.

Luke:

"You tired?"

Mark:

"Yeah, it's been a long day."

Luke:

"It was great looking at the Kwaj pictures with you, remembering fun times we've had together."

Mark:

"For me too, Luke."

Luke:

"I'm working tomorrow afternoon in the grocery store. Other than that, why don't we play things by ear. Don't want to overload you."

Mark:

"I appreciate it. It's much different from Kwaj, but I'm enjoying it."

Luke:

"That's good. I wasn't sure how you'd feel, as it's been a while since we've hung out."

Mark:

"I'm not totally comfortable, but I'm getting there."

Luke:

"Cool."

Luke turns off the light, and they both lie awake without talking, finding good sleeping positions. As their breathing slows, Mark falls asleep first, worn out from the past two days of travel. Excited about Mark's arrival, Luke lies awake looking at the ceiling. Luke notices Mark's snoring, briefly looks over at him and smiles. Luke then turns to the wall, closes his eyes and falls into a deep, contented slumber.

Chapter 2

Unlike most days, Luke's 20-year-old brother, Ricky, is up early, excited about his team's soccer match in a few hours.

His room is on the first floor across from the kitchen and messy, with dirty clothes strewn next to an unused hamper, his double bed unmade and the top of his dresser piled with his wallet and keys, cigarettes and lighter, a pot pipe and issues of *Surfer* and *World Soccer* magazines. Ricky's dry wet suit hangs from a bedpost. His soccer cleats, shin guards and knee-high socks stick out from under the bed on one side, and his surfboard's fin and ankle leash are visible on the other.

Ricky wears only green soccer shorts and is combing his shoulder-length dark-blond hair, sun-bleached from surfing and soccer. He is just under five foot six with a wiry, muscular build.

There are two motorcycle helmets on the floor next to his bedroom door. Surfing music plays on his stereo.

He puts on his white-and-green-striped soccer jersey, places the rest of his uniform in his motorcycle backpack next to the bedroom door, picks up the latest issue of *Surfer* magazine and lies on his bed to read an article on surfing Oahu's North Shore, an area known for its big waves with challenging barrels that make it less crowded than other Hawaiian surfing spots.

Ricky hears a knock on his closed door.

Ricky:

"Yeah?"

Luke:

"Breakfast is ready."

Ricky:

"Be out in a minute."

Luke goes back into the kitchen, joining Mark at the table. Luke's mom has made waffles, bacon and eggs, which are warming in the oven, and she moves them to the table as she joins the boys to eat.

Luke:

"Anything in particular you want to do today, Mark?"

Mark:

"Hang out with you."

Luke:

"I'm working this afternoon at the grocery store, but we'll spend the rest of the day together."

Mark:

"Great."

Ricky sits at the table and starts drinking the coffee he poured at the stove.

Luke's mom:

"Luke, why don't you two go pick some strawberries."

Luke and Mark go out the back door and stop to put on flip-flops lined up on the landing. As they approach the garden, Mark sees the strawberry plants are heavy with ripe, red fruit. The boys pick the ripest ones, holding them in impromptu pouches they've made using the front of their T-shirts. As they gather the fruit, they sample it.

Mark:

"These are good."

Luke nods in agreement, as he savors the juicy sweetness.

After filling their pouches, they go inside and release the fruit into a metal colander in the sink. Luke rinses and dries the strawberries and brings them to the table, and the four of them enjoy the meal.

Ricky:

"I'm leaving for my soccer game after breakfast."

Luke:

"Can we come watch?"

Ricky:

"Why not?"

Luke's mom:

"Just be careful."

Luke:

"We will."

After breakfast, Mark and Luke sit together on Luke's bed as they put on socks and sneakers.

Luke:

"Did you sleep okay?"

Mark:

"Yeah, I needed it. Was pretty wiped out."

Luke:

"I could tell."

The two go out back and see Ricky on his motorcycle next to the garage. Wearing a matching black leather jacket and motorcycle boots, he puts on his helmet and starts up the bike.

Ricky:

"See you guys there."

He rides down the driveway to the street, taking a right toward the high school.

Luke and Mark get their bikes out of the open garage and head off in the same direction. They go by a neighbor cutting his lawn, and from behind the yard's fence his cairn terrier lets out his fiercest guard-dog bark.

Mark:

"Hey, Toto."

The neighbor waves, and the three share a laugh.

The early-morning weather couldn't be better, and the two enjoy riding together through the neighborhood's peaceful streets.

As they reach the high school, they spot Ricky, his teammates and the opposing team warming up. Ricky is now in his full soccer regalia. Some teammates are stretching or jogging up and down the field. Others are paired off, kicking balls back and forth. Ricky, the team's star forward, is launching well-aimed missiles that elude their goalie's long arms and hit their mark inside the goal.

An umpire in a black-and-white shirt and black pants walks to the center of the field and blows his whistle. The two teams quickly move their practice equipment to the sidelines and position themselves for the game's start.

The umpire throws the first ball high in the air, and the two centers scuffle to gain control of it. Ricky's team member wins the contest, and the ball heads toward the opposition's goal. The ball reaches Ricky, and he expertly maneuvers it in and out of the opposing team's defense, punting it to one of his teammates, who rapidly returns it to Ricky, who is now directly in front of the goal. Ricky pulls his leg back and kicks the ball high and to the right. The goalie stretches to block the shot, but the ball glances off his fingertips and slaps the back of the net.

Luke and Mark are standing on the sidelines watching, and they jump up and down when Ricky makes the goal.

Luke:

"Way to go, Ricky!"

Ricky waves at his brother and high-fives several of his teammates. The excitement dies down, and the game goes on.

Mark:

"Luke, have you played any soccer since you left Kwaj?"

Luke:

"Some, mainly during PE. I'm not as good as Ricky."

Mark:

"The only team sport I play is inner tube water polo. Otherwise, I stick to running, swimming and tennis."

Luke:

"Do you still run barefoot?"

Mark:

"No, after you left, I started wearing Pumas. What about you?"

Luke:

"I wear Nikes now when I run on the track team."

Mark and Luke turn their attention back to the game. Ricky competes aggressively, and his love of soccer shines through in his face and movements, his long hair blowing back as he runs.

Luke:

"I'm getting thirsty. You want some water?"

Mark nods.

Luke and Mark make their way over to a guy selling drinks out of several large coolers.

Drink vendor:

"What can I get you guys?"

Luke:

"Two waters."

The vendor opens a cooler, sticks his arm in the ice and pulls out two bottles, handing them to Luke:

"One dollar."

Luke hands him the money.

Drink vendor:

"Thanks."

Luke:

"Here, Mark."

Mark:

"Thanks."

The two walk back to their place on the sidelines, as Ricky attempts another goal. The goalie catches this one and throws the ball downfield.

Mark:

"What's your job like?"

Luke:

"I bag groceries, stock shelves, clean and whatever else the store manager needs. The best part is getting my weekly paycheck."

Mark:

"I'm lifeguarding at the pool and Emon Beach."

Luke:

"How's that?"

Mark:

"Sometimes boring, but I like it. When I'm up in the lifeguard stand at the beach, I listen to Casey Kasem's American Top 40 on my radio. Helps pass the time."

The opposing team scores the game-winning goal, and the two teams line up facing one another and shake hands. Afterward, Ricky jogs up to Luke and Mark.

Luke:

"Sorry you guys lost."

Ricky:

"Yeah, it sucks."

Luke:

"We're heading back."

Ricky:

"I'm gonna hang out for a bit."

Ricky and his teammates put their gear in white mesh bags while they talk and drink water.

Ricky:

"We'll get them next time."

Teammate:

"Great goal, Ricky."

Ricky:

"Thanks."

Ricky changes into his riding outfit:

"I'll catch you guys later."

While he heads home on his motorcycle, Ricky replays the game in his head, strategizing what he'll do differently next time.

Luke and Mark are putting their bikes away, as Ricky turns into the driveway.

Luke:

"Mark, let's go upstairs, so I can change for work."

Mark sits on his bed, his back against the wall, discretely admiring Luke as he strips down to his boxer shorts, puts on his grocery-store uniform and pulls his hair into a ponytail.

Mark:

"I'll probably explore the neighborhood on my bike while you're at work."

Luke:

"I'll be back late this afternoon."

They walk down to the kitchen, where Luke's mom is scrubbing the inside of the oven.

Luke:

"Mom, I'm off to work."

Mark:

"I'm going for a bike ride."

Luke's mom:

"Be careful, boys."

They ride together on their bikes. It's midday, sunny and warm. The blue sky is punctuated with drifting white cumulus clouds. Their pace is easy. Mark takes in the neighborhood's sights: curving tree-lined streets dappled with sunlight, a group of children playing driveway kickball, an on-foot postman delivering mail house by house.

Luke:

"My turn's here."

Mark:

"See ya later."

Mark continues straight. A while later, the trees and houses start to thin out, and the road becomes hilly. Mark glides down the hills and pumps his legs to get up them. He then comes to a long, steep downhill, with grassy banks on either side. The bike accelerates. At first, Mark enjoys the speed, but then he begins to squeeze the hand brakes to slow down. He discovers they're not working, and pumping them does no good.

Mark:

"Shit."

Scared, he sees a group of tall bushes at the bottom of the hill. Mark braces himself, steers into them and is caught by the prickly plants. He lies still for a minute, breathes a sigh of relief and extricates himself. He assesses the damage and sees the bike is fine. For the most part, he is unharmed, but his arms are dirty, scratched and bleeding.

He pulls off his T-shirt to tend his arms as best as he can and sits on the roadside to calm down. Mark looks at the eagles soaring above and ponders what to do next.

He remembers he's near Luke's work, puts on his bloodied T-shirt and starts riding toward downtown Santa Cruz, walking the bike down the hills and riding up them.

As Mark enters the downtown area, he sees the streets are lined with small businesses – a hardware store, a crafts shop and a post office, as well as restaurants and bars with a smattering of customers. Cars occupy some of the parallel parking spaces.

Mark spots Luke's grocery store, locks his bike next to it and enters via the glass doors. The store is narrow and deep. Customers are selecting their items from high, tightly packed shelves and loading their shopping carts. Some wait at the deli counter in the back right corner as two clerks fill orders for cold cuts and store-made coleslaw and potato salad.

Mark sees Luke, who is brown-bagging a customer's groceries at a front checkout register. He forgets about the accident as he once more appreciates how Luke looks in his uniform. Luke looks up, sees Mark walking toward him and smiles. His smile turns to a look of concern when he notices the blood on Mark's T-shirt and the cuts and dirt on his arms.

Luke:

"What happened?"

Mark:

"The bike's brakes gave out when I was going down a hill. I had to use bushes to stop."

Luke:

"You all right?"

Mark:

"Just shaken up."

Luke:

"You had me worried."

Mark:

"Didn't do such a good job cleaning up."

Luke talks to the store manager next to him. The manager nods.

Luke:

"Follow me, Mark."

They walk down an aisle and through a set of swinging doors into the stockroom. The area is windowless, with stark overhead lighting. Gray metal shelving runs to the ceiling and is heavy with items still in shipping boxes. Luke rolls a wide stepladder over to Mark.

"Sit here."

As Mark sits, Luke takes first-aid supplies off a shelf.

Mark holds out his hand.

Luke:

"Let me."

Luke soaks a few cotton balls in hydrogen peroxide and gently cleans the cuts on Mark's upper right arm. Mark winces, and Luke stops.

Mark:

"Stings some."

Luke smiles, nods and finishes cleaning the arm. He then dabs some antibiotic ointment on the cuts and wraps them with a gauze bandage.

Mark gratefully watches Luke as he repeats the process on Mark's left arm.

Mark:

"Thanks. That helps."

Luke:

"Of course. I need to get back to bagging though."

They walk back to the front.

Luke:

"I'll be home in a while."

As Mark goes outside, he squints from the bright sun, retrieves his bike and rides back to Luke's house. He enters through the kitchen, where he stops for a large glass of ice-cold water. No one else is home. Mark goes upstairs, lies on his bed and falls asleep, exhausted.

Mark wakes up when Luke comes in the bedroom.

Luke:

"Hey, sleepyhead."

Mark:

"What time is it?"

Luke:

"Dinnertime."

Mark:

"Good. I'm hungry."

Luke goes first, and as they walk down the steps, Mark puts his hands on Luke's shoulders. They stop for a moment, Luke smiles up at Mark and they continue down.

As they enter the kitchen, Luke's mom is putting dinner on the table, where Luke's dad and Ricky are seated. The table setting includes glass drinking cups that originally contained sour cream. Each is adorned with multicolor flowers. Dinner consists of roasted chicken, already carved and piled high on a serving platter, steamed corn on the cob and artichokes, sliced wheat bread, green bean casserole and coleslaw.

Luke's dad:

"Mom, you've outdone yourself again."

Luke's mom:

"Thanks, Don."

The family fills their plates.

Ricky:

"I scored two goals today, but we lost."

Luke's dad:

"Better luck next time."

Ricky:

"What we need is to tighten up our defense."

Luke's mom:

"Luke told us about your accident, Mark. How are you, honey?"

Mark:

"I'm fine. Luke helped me clean up at his store."

Ricky:

"Awww. Isn't that sweet."

Luke:

"Ricky, quit it!"

Luke's dad:

"Luke, why don't you and Mark come with me to work tomorrow. It'll be Saturday, the high school will be quiet, and you can help me out."

Luke:

"Sure, dad."

Mark:

"I've never had steamed artichokes before. How do you eat them?"

Luke's dad demonstrates as he explains:

"Put a tablespoon of mayo on your plate next to the artichoke. Pull off a leaf and dip it in the mayo. Use your teeth to strip off the meat."

Mark:

"Pretty good."

Luke's dad smiles at Mark.

The family continues to discuss the day's activities and finish dinner. Afterward, Luke and Mark help Luke's mom with the dishes.

Luke:

"Mom, we're going to head on up."

Luke's mom hugs them:

"Sleep well, you two."

Luke and Mark go into the darkened bedroom. Luke turns on the nightstand light, and they change into gym shorts. The two go into the bathroom and brush their teeth, standing side by side at the sink.

Luke:

"It was quite a day."

Mark:

"Definitely."

They cross back to the bedroom and get into bed.

Luke:

"I'm glad you stopped at the store for help."

Mark:

"Your boss didn't mind?"

Luke:

"He was fine. It didn't take too long. After we help my dad tomorrow, I was thinking we'd swing by Stef's to hang out."

As Luke mentions his girlfriend, Mark is jealous of her.

Luke:

"The three of us can also go to the beach and boardwalk one day this week. They have good rides."

Mark:

"Sounds fun."

They lie quiet for a while, comfortable together. The silence is broken only by the chirping of crickets and the buzz of the streetlight. Luke looks over at Mark, who is almost asleep. He reaches out and touches Mark's shoulder.

Luke:

"Night, Mark."

Mark:

"Good night, Luke."

Chapter 3

Luke is awakened by sunlight streaming through the dormer windows. He opens his eyes, stretches and looks at the nightstand clock, which says 7 a.m. He turns on his side, propping himself up on his elbow, and looks over at Mark, who is still asleep, facing the wall.

Luke:

"Hey, Mark. Time to get up to help my dad at work."

Mark turns over and groggily looks at Luke.

Luke:

"It's supposed to be kind of cold, so put on something warm."

Mark:

"Okay."

Mark goes to his end of the closet and takes out a pair of white briefs, jeans, a blue T-shirt and a red hoodie.

Mark:

"I'm gonna get a shower."

Luke:

"I'll take one after you."

As Mark heads into the bathroom, Luke gets faded overalls and a white T-shirt from the dresser and puts a blue windbreaker from the closet on his bed. When Luke enters the bathroom, Mark is already in the shower. Luke begins brushing his teeth at the sink as he watches himself in the mirror.

Luke:

"How'd you sleep?"

Mark:

"Pretty good. You?"

Luke:

"Same."

Mark turns off the water, pulls open the curtain and reaches for the towel hanging next to him. Luke glances over at Mark's naked body. While drying off, Mark briefly returns Luke's gaze as he tucks the towel around his waist.

Luke finishes brushing his teeth, takes off his gym shorts and boxers and switches positions with Mark. Luke turns the shower back on, tests the water temperature and steps into the shower as Mark brushes his teeth and gets dressed.

Luke turns off the shower and dries himself. As Mark finishes putting on his shoes, he looks at Luke from time to time as Luke gets dressed.

Mark:

"I'll meet you downstairs."

Luke:

"K."

When Mark goes into the kitchen, Luke's dad is making coffee and toasting bread for them.

Luke's dad:

"Morning."

Mark:

"Morning."

The silver percolator sits on a lit gas stove burner, the coffee bubbling up in its clear-glass top. Luke's dad is dressed in his olive-green uniform with "Janitor" embroidered on the left breast pocket.

Luke's dad:

"We're going to keep things simple, coffee and toast, so we can head out."

Luke's dad turns off the burner, gets out three off-white coffee mugs, pours a cup for himself and takes two pieces of toast from the stack he's made. He sits at the kitchen table and reads the morning paper as he eats.

Mark gets himself breakfast, spreading butter and jam on his toast, and joins Luke's dad at the table.

Luke's dad:

"As soon as Luke gets something to eat, we'll head over to the high school."

Once the three are done eating and cleaning up, they head out to the garage, from which Luke's dad retrieves his metal toolbox and puts it in the back of the truck.

They climb in the truck, with Luke in the center and Mark on the passenger side, and Luke's dad pulls the truck out of the garage and stops.

Luke's dad:

"Mark, can you close the garage door?"

Mark:

"Sure."

Mark climbs out, shuts the garage door and gets back in. When the truck gets to the end of the driveway, Luke's dad turns right, heading toward the high school.

Luke's dad:

"I'm going to have you guys help me with the boy's locker room today."

Luke's dad turns on a country music station as they come to a four-way stop.

Luke:

"My Aunt Rachel lives two blocks that way."

Mark:

"How often do you see her?"

Luke:

"Every other Sunday, when we go over for dinner. When the weather's nice, we barbeque."

In 10 minutes, Luke's dad pulls into the school's side parking lot and parks next to a storage building where his office and equipment-and-supply area are located.

Luke's dad:

"Luke, can you get the toolbox out of the back?"

Luke:

"K."

Mark follows Luke's dad inside his office, followed by Luke, who struggles with the toolbox's weight but manages. Luke's dad opens the box and takes out the needed tools.

Luke's dad:

"Follow me."

They go into the storage area next to the office.

Luke's dad:

"Boys, grab a bucket, cleaning rags and Pine-sol. I'll get the painting stuff."

Mark and Luke find their items, while Luke's dad gathers a gallon of light-blue paint, brushes, sandpaper, a scraper and a folded canvas drop cloth that looks like an unframed Jackson Pollock painting. They exit the storage area and go into the main school building, passing through a classroom hallway lined with lockers.

Luke:

"I take chemistry in there."

Mark peers into the room through the door's viewing pane and sees rows of chemistry workbenches. Each bench has a sink and two high stools and is populated with glass beakers and test tubes, Bunsen burners, and microscopes that all together look like a miniature city skyline.

Mark:

"Cool."

As they near the indoor basketball court next to the boys' locker room where they will be working, the three pass a display cabinet with championship trophies and action photographs of the school's past star athletes.

Luke:

"Mark, look, there's Ricky running on the soccer field his senior year."

Mark:

"Wow."

They turn into the boys' locker room, which has painted cinderblock walls and green metal lockers.

Luke's dad:

"We're going to focus on the walls and lockers in here today. I need to have you guys start with the lockers."

Luke:

"What do you want us to do?"

Luke's dad:

"Put hot water and Pine-sol in the bucket. Then with rags, wipe down and dry the lockers inside and out. I'm going to paint the walls."

The yellow wheeled bucket is one Luke's dad uses to mop the school floors, and Luke fills it halfway with hot water at the utility sink and adds a healthy dose of the cleaning fluid. Two parallel rows of lockers line the walls of the locker room, and Mark and Luke work across from one another.

As they do this, Luke's dad scrapes loose paint off the walls, sands rough spots and brushes on a coat of paint. Midway, he pauses and looks at the boys' work.

"You guys are doing a great job."

Several hours later, he inspects the results of all their efforts.

"It looks great. You two were a big help. Let's call it a day."

The three gather up the supplies, walk back to the storage area and put things away. Luke's dad locks everything up, and they go home.

As Luke's dad turns into the driveway and parks the truck inside the garage, they see Ricky lying on the ground, repairing his motorcycle engine. Tools lay next to him.

Luke's dad:

"How's it going?"

Ricky:

"Fine. I'm changing the oil, air filter and spark plugs."

The three go inside, and a bit later Luke and Mark go back out to sit on the porch and drink orange sodas while they watch Ricky fix his bike.

Mark:

"We still going to Stephanie's this afternoon?"

Luke:

"I'll call her in a little to check."

Ricky finishes and puts his tools away in the garage. He gets on the motorcycle, jumps on the pedals and the engine roars to life.

Ricky:

"You guys want to go for a spin with me?"

Luke:

"I'm scared of that thing."

Ricky:

"Come on, Luke. Grow a pair."

Luke:

"No way."

Ricky:

"Bawk, bawk, bawk, bawk. Someone's a chicken."

Luke:

"Okay, but you've got to take it easy."

Ricky:

"K."

Leaving the bike running, Ricky puts the kickstand down and gets the motorcycle helmets from his bedroom and hands Luke one.

Luke struggles to put on the helmet, and Ricky helps him.

Ricky:

"Like this."

Ricky secures his own helmet and gets back on the bike, and Luke climbs on behind him.

Ricky:

"Put your feet here."

Luke does as told and wraps his arms around his brother's waist. Ricky drives to the street, turns left and quickly accelerates. Mark runs down the driveway behind them and watches as they ride away.

Ricky and Luke go from tree-lined streets to a deserted two-lane road, with Luke hanging on for dear life. Behind his wind visor, Luke's face is contorted in fear. Ricky smiles behind his. After a short while, Ricky makes a U-turn and returns home. When they get back, Mark is sitting on the back steps.

Ricky brings the bike to a stop, and Luke jumps off.

Mark:

"How was it, Luke?"

Luke:

"Scary, but not too bad."

Ricky:

"Okay, Mahte. Your turn."

Mark:

"I don't know."

Ricky:

"Bawk, bawk, bawk."

Luke:

"Ricky, stop."

Ricky:

"C'mon. If Luke can do it, you can."

Mark:

"All right."

Luke passes the helmet to Mark, who climbs on, and Luke watches them leave. When they return, Mark says, "That's the last time I'm getting on a motorcycle."

Ricky:

"I'm impressed you guys tried it."

They go inside, Ricky to his bedroom while Luke and Mark stay in the kitchen. Mark sits at the table, and Luke calls Stephanie on a yellow wall-mounted rotary phone with a long spiral cord.

Luke:

"Hey, Mrs. Russo. It's Luke."

Mrs. Russo:

"Hello, Luke."

Luke:

"Is Stephanie there?"

Mrs. Russo:

"Yes, she's right here. Let me put her on."

Stephanie:

"Hey, Luke."

Luke:

"Hey Stef, how's it goin'?"

Stephanie:

"Pretty good. Just talking with mom."

Luke:

"Still okay if Mark and I come over to hang out?"

Stephanie:

"That would be great. The rest of the gang is coming over too."

Luke:

"Cool. We'll be there in about half an hour."

Luke and Mark go up to the bedroom, and Luke gets two backpacks from the upper closet shelf for them.

Luke:

"Let's put on our suits here. Why don't you get towels from the bathroom."

The boys get changed and put towels and an extra set of clothes in their backpacks.

As they walk through the kitchen to get their bikes, Luke's

mom is baking carrot cake.

Luke:

"We're goin' over to Stef's."

Luke's mom:

"Have fun."

The bike ride takes them into the adjoining neighborhood

where Stephanie lives. The houses are more affluent and set

farther apart. A number of them have pools.

Luke and Mark arrive at the Russo's and prop their bikes on the side of the house, just outside the chain-link fence around the house's backyard.

They go through the gate into the backyard, where Stephanie and a group of their friends are relaxing on the cement deck or in the in-ground pool. Stephanie is on a lounge chair and gets up when she sees them. She is 17, cute, her light-brown hair cut in a Dorothy Hamill bob. She is several inches taller than Luke and gives him a quick kiss on the cheek. She is wearing short cutoff jeans slightly frayed at the bottom and a red bikini top.

Luke:

"This is Mark."

Stephanie:

"Nice to finally meet you, Mark."

Mark:

"You too."

Some of the teenagers are playing pool volleyball.

Luke and Mark take off their shirts and put their backpacks on a chair, as Stephanie takes off her shorts, revealing a matching bikini bottom. She sits back down and starts rubbing suntan lotion on her arms, stomach and legs. She unhooks the back of her bikini top.

Stephanie:

"Luke, can you put lotion on my back?"

Luke sits next to her, takes the lotion and squirts some on her back, massaging it into her shoulders and lower back.

Stephanie:

"That feels good. You're the best."

Luke moves to the chair next to Stephanie's, and as they sunbathe, they hold hands.

Mark is now sitting at the edge of the pool, dangling his legs in the water. He is agitated watching Luke and Stephanie, so he decides to join the volleyball game. With his focus on the game, Mark relaxes and enjoys himself.

When Mark's team wins, the game breaks up. Some players get out of the pool and a few stay in, including Mark.

Mark:

"Let's play Marco Polo."

This grabs Luke's attention, and he and Stephanie get up from their lounge chairs to join in the new game.

Mark:

"I'll be Marco to start."

Mark closes his eyes, and Stephanie spins him around several times to disorient him. The others in the pool move away from Mark to the pool's outer edges.

Mark:

"Marco."

The others:

"Polo."

Mark:

"Marco."

The others:

"Polo."

Mark picks up on Luke's voice and begins moving toward

him.

Mark:

"Marco."

Luke:

"Polo."

Mark closes in on Luke, who is trying to get away but quickly losing ground.

Mark:

"Marco."

Luke:

"Polo."

Mark reaches Luke, grabs him from behind and playfully hugs him. The two briefly go underwater together and emerge separate once Luke breaks free. They surface laughing and shaking the water from their eyes and hair. Stephanie watches this give and take, noting the two's closeness.

The game ends, and the group in the pool swim and lie on plastic floats. Mark and Luke engage in a friendly diving and flipping contest on the diving board.

Mrs. Russo calls out from the kitchen window overlooking the pool:

"Kids, the food's ready."

The teenagers stop what they're doing and make their way inside. They put hamburgers, hot dogs and potato chips on paper plates and go back outside. While eating, they talk, laugh and listen to music.

After lunch, Luke changes into dry clothes in the bathroom next to the kitchen. Once he's done, Mark also changes.

Luke:

"Stef, we're going to head home now."

Stephanie:

"You want me to walk you guys out?"

Luke kisses Stephanie on the cheek.

Luke:

"No, we're fine."

Mark:

"Nice meeting you, Stephanie."

Stephanie:

"You too, Mark. Bye, guys."

After getting home and putting their bikes away, Luke and Mark go inside to the kitchen, where Luke's mom and dad are sitting at the table drinking coffee and eating the homemade carrot cake.

Luke's mom:

"How was Stef's?"

Luke:

"We had fun."

Luke's mom:

"You hungry?"

Luke:

"Nah, we had a lot there. We're gonna head up for the night."

Luke's dad:

"Sleep well."

Mark and Luke climb the stairs slower than usual, worn out from the day's activities.

Luke switches on the nightstand light as they enter the room. They take off their backpacks, leaving the unpacking until the next morning, and climb into bed.

Mark:

"It was quite a day."

Luke:

"Agree."

Mark:

"I really enjoyed our diving competition."

Luke:

"Yeah, it was fun. Can't believe you caught me in Marco Polo. Tomorrow should be a good day for the beach. There's also a boardwalk there, where we can hang out in the evening and go on some rides."

Mark:

"Cool. Good night."

Luke:

"Sweet dreams."

Luke turns out the light, and they both stare at the darkened ceiling, replaying the day in their heads until sleep overtakes them.

Chapter 4

As Luke had predicted, the day was ideal for the beach and boardwalk. Lying in bed, Mark watched the sky go from black to navy blue to baby blue.

Luke began to show signs of life.

Mark:

"Morning."

Luke:

"Hey, you."

Mark:

"How did you sleep?"

Luke:

"Ask me when I'm actually awake."

Mark:

"I've been thinking about what today might be like."

Luke:

"We'll have fun. We'll go in bathing suits and T-shirts to the beach and bring clothes for the boardwalk."

Mark:

"Okay."

Luke:

"They have outdoor showers next to the bathrooms."

Mark:

"Great. I hate the itchy feel of dry salt on my skin."

Luke:

"Make sure to pack a sweatshirt. It'll get cold tonight, especially with the wind at the top of the Ferris wheel. That reminds me … I need to call Stef to see if she's still going."

Mark hopes that she isn't.

The boys get ready and head down for breakfast. Luke finds a note from his mom on the refrigerator:

"Honey,

Aunt Rachel and I are at the flea market buying furniture for her sunporch. Dad's working.

Have a good time today.

Love, Mom

P.S. There's eggs and hash browns on the stove."

Luke goes to the stove, uncovers the frying pan and gets two plates.

Luke:

"Mark, can ya go pick some strawberries?"

Mark nods, grabs an empty bowl and heads out to the garden while Luke divides up the food onto the plates and warms it up in the microwave.

Once they finish eating, Mark cleans up while Luke calls Stephanie.

Luke:

"Hi, Mr. Russo. It's Luke. Is Stef there?"

Stephanie's dad:

"Morning, Luke. Let me get her."

Stephanie:

"Hey, Luke."

Luke:

"Hey. Did your folks say it'd be okay for you to spend the day with us?"

Stephanie:

"Yeah, I'll meet you at the beach around 11. My mom's going to drop me off."

Luke:

"Cool. We'll set up near the lifeguard station. If we're not sitting with our stuff, it means we're either in the water or walking on the beach."

Stephanie:

"K. See ya soon."

Luke:

"Bye."

Luke:

"Let's head out."

The two put on their backpacks, get their bikes from the garage and start to ride. After leaving Luke's neighborhood, they go through downtown Santa Cruz and arrive at the boardwalk alongside the beach, and find a bike rack to secure their bikes.

Luke:

"Look, Mark. You can see the Ferris wheel at the other end of the boardwalk. That's where the other rides are too."

Mark:

"Oh, yeah. It towers over everything."

Luke and Mark take off their sneakers and socks, shove them into mesh pockets on the sides of their backpacks and walk down the boardwalk steps to the beach.

The Santa Cruz beach is wide and stretches out in both directions, well beyond the boardwalk. The sand crunches under the boys' feet as they walk to the lifeguard stand. The beach is sparsely populated midmorning.

As they walk, Luke looks at the ocean and sees a group of surfers several hundred yards out. They are wearing full-body wetsuits to guard against the ocean's cold, which has come from the Arctic, and are on their surfboards lying on their stomachs or kneeling as they bob up and down watching for incoming waves.

Luke:

"I can tell that's Ricky from his hair and wetsuit pattern."

Luke and Mark wave to Ricky, who sees them and waves back.

Mark:

"How often does he go out?"

Luke:

"A few times a week with his buddies. He started doing it in high school."

The two walk past the lifeguard stand and stop after passing a group of teenagers camped out with towels and beach chairs and umbrellas offering respite from the California sun.

Luke:

"Let's set up here."

They put down their backpacks, spread out towels and take off their T-shirts.

Luke:

"C'mon. Let's get in."

They go down to the water and wade in up to their ankles.

Mark:

"You didn't tell me it was going to be so cold!"

Luke:

"I wanted you to discover that on your own."

Mark:

"It's late June. Shouldn't it be warm?"

Luke:

"Comes from Artic. Never warms up. That's why Ricky and his buddies wear wetsuits."

Mark and Luke stay at the water's edge, watching Ricky and his friends as they spot a good wave, paddle furiously to catch the surge and ride it to the shore. After a while, the boys go in up to their waists, and Luke dives in. Mark watches, shaking his head, but finally does the same. Luke is treading water, watching for Mark, who quickly emerges.

"It's so cold it took my breath away."

Luke:

"Swim around. It may help."

The two swim closer to the surfers, who catch one wave after another, sometimes making it all the way to the shore.

Mark:

"I have to go back to the beach. My body is numb."

Luke:

"Me too."

They use their towels to dry off and then lie on them to warm up in the sun.

Mark:

"I've never been in water that cold."

Luke:

Luke:

"It takes some getting used to."

As Luke looks up at the broad expanse of sky, Stephanie comes into view, wearing a blue bikini top with cutoff jeans. They smile at each other.

Stephanie:

"How's it hangin'?"

Luke:

"We're warmin' up. We just got out."

Mark:

"I froze my you-know-whats off!"

Stephanie sets her things next to Luke and does a little dance as she steps out of her cutoffs to catch Luke's attention. Luke smiles at her as she spreads out her towel and sits on it. Stephanie next retrieves suntan lotion from her backpack and generously rubs it on her arms, legs and stomach. Luke watches as she slathers it on and then hands him the bottle.

Stephanie:

"Can you?"

Luke:

"Sure."

He squirts lotion on her shoulders and lower back, rubbing it in until her skin has absorbed it.

Stephanie:

"Thanks, babe."

Mark is sitting up on his towel, watching as the beach fills with swimmers and sunbathers. From time to time, he steals glances at Luke and Stephanie's interactions. Stephanie gets granola bars from her backpack for the three of them.

As they snack, Ricky comes out of the water with two other surfers. As they walk, the three pull the top half of their wetsuits off their arms and torsos, letting the suits hang like a snake in the middle of shedding its skin. Each carries his board by his side.

Ricky:

"Hey, guys."

Luke:

"How were the waves?"

Ricky:

"We got in some good rides. Right, guys?"

Ricky's two companions nod.

Ricky:

"Did you see me wipe out?"

Luke:

"It looked painful."

Ricky:

"Gotta have a thick skin to get through life, bro. We'll catch ya later."

By early afternoon, the trio wanted to eat something more substantial than the granola bars.

Luke:

"Why don't we pack up and head to the bathrooms to get changed so we can catch some lunch and rides on the boardwalk."

They make their way over to the bathrooms and use the outdoor showers to clean up before heading inside to put on dry clothes.

The inside of the men's bathroom has urinals and bathroom stalls off to the right and an open area with benches to the left. Luke and Mark go to an open bench to change, as other teen boys and a number of young fathers help their small sons do the same. Luke and Mark look at each other intermittently as they strip off their wet suits and put on clean clothes.

Luke:

"Let's not wait until tonight to go on the rides. We'll do it after lunch."

Mark:

"Sounds good. But I have to warn you: I need time to digest my food. When my dad took our family to Disney World last summer, we went on the Matterhorn bobsleds and the jerking motions in the dark got me pretty queasy."

Luke:

"Okay, after eating, we'll play some arcade games and then go on milder rides like the Ferris wheel before doing the roller coaster."

Mark gives Luke a thumbs-up.

The two finish changing and leave the men's room as Stephanie exits the women's room wearing a yellow-and-white sundress and flat sandals. Lockers line the wall outside the restrooms, and they put their backpacks in one, lock it and look for a place to eat on the boardwalk.

After passing several food stands, they settle on hot dogs, french fries with vinegar, and soda. They sit on a white wooden bench with a movable back, which they position so they can watch the parade of people as they eat.

Stephanie:

"Mark, what do you think of Santa Cruz?"

Mark:

"I like it. It's beautiful. Mainly, it's been great to hang out with Luke again."

Stephanie:

"Yeah, he hasn't had much time for me since you arrived."

Luke:

"Stef, you know Mark's only here for a short time. And I have to work."

Stephanie:

"Yeah. I didn't really mean it."

Luke:

"Then why say it?"

Stephanie:

"The bitch in me came out for a sec."

Luke:

"I'm glad we haven't seen her for a while."

Stephanie:

"Me too."

Luke:

"We'll have more time later after Mark goes back to Kwaj."

Mark feels bad about the tension he's caused between Luke and Stephanie and decides to talk about it with Luke later. For now, he focuses on eating and observing the families and teenagers walking by.

After throwing out their trash, the three walk over to the nearby game arcade.

Luke:

"How 'bout some air hockey?"

Stephanie:

"I get to beat you first."

Luke laughs.

"Don't be so sure of yourself."

When they get inside, Mark goes to the change machine.

"Let me get this one."

The first time he puts a $10 bill from his wallet into the machine, it doesn't accept it. So he smooths the bill on his leg and tries again. The machine grabs the money and five seconds later spits out quarters into the metal cup like a Las Vegas slot machine paying out a winning spin.

Mark divides the quarters into thirds and hands Luke and Stephanie theirs. Stephanie goes to the air hockey game, and she and Luke start a friendly competition while Mark watches.

Mark loses interest in the rivalry after Stephanie scores the first two goals, and he starts looking around. His attention is caught by an Elton John Pinball Wizard machine, from the movie *Tommy* that The Who had released the previous summer. Mark had seen it while his dad and sister Michele had watched *Jaws* in the theater next to his.

Mark:

"I'm going to play some pinball."

Luke scores a goal.

"We'll be over once I win."

Stephanie:

"No, you mean after I trounce you."

Mark leaves the two to continue duking it out and makes his way to the pinball machine.

Mark enjoys playing pinball, and once their quarters run out, the three head over to the Ferris wheel.

As it's early afternoon, the line is short, and the three are soon squeezed into one car with Stephanie in the center. After the operator finishes loading the other cars, their ride begins. Each time their car reaches the top, Luke points out Santa Cruz landmarks.

Luke:

"The rest of downtown is off to the right. See the grocery store where I work?"

Mark:

"Oh, yeah. How did you get that job?"

Luke:

"A friend of mine who works there told the manager I was interested."

Mark:

"How long have you been doing it?"

Luke:

"A year. It's great getting the paychecks. A couple of miles outside of town that way is the Mystery Spot."

Mark:

"Where?"

Luke:

"Over there, where the redwood forest is."

Mark:

"What is it?"

Luke:

"When you go inside its cabins, you see strange things. The people look like they are walking almost sideways, and golf balls roll uphill."

Mark:

"For real?"

Luke:

"Would I kid you?"

Mark:

"Yes."

As the boys talk, Stephanie sees the strong connection, which she tries to block.

Stephanie:

"Mark, if you look in the same direction as Luke's grocery store, you can see my house farther out."

Mark:

"How can I tell which one it is?"

Stephanie:

"It's an L with a kidney-shaped pool."

Next are the bumper cars, where they each get their own car. As they drive around the oval rink, they enjoy ramming into each other.

Their last ride is Santa Cruz's historic wooden roller coaster, the Giant Dipper. Built in the mid-1920s, it's one of the world's most popular wooden coasters, with a 70-foot plunge and many tight turns. Luke and Stephanie ride together, and Mark sits behind them on his own. The ride's gyrations are too much for Mark, and afterward he tells Luke:

"The roller coaster did a number on my stomach."

Just as he says "stomach," Mark's face goes white and his stomach cramps up. He desperately looks around. His eyes lock on the round metal trash can to his left. Its top is open, and the can is half full of the day's refuse. Mark leans forward with his face close to the opening and explosively vomits. Only when his stomach is empty does his heaving stop.

Luke:

"C'mon Mark. Let's get you cleaned up."

Luke stretches out his arm, and Mark leans into Luke's shoulder for support, as they make their way to the men's room near the roller coaster. Stephanie walks on Mark's other side, ready to help if needed and waits on the boardwalk when they go in.

Inside is a row of white porcelain sinks. They go to the nearest one. Luke opens up the hot and cold water taps and puts in the tan plastic stopper. Mark scoops water out of the filled sink with his cupped hands, splashing it on his face and neck and also gets his hair, upper chest and arms wet in the process. As color returns to his face, Mark woozily looks at himself in the mirror and then at Luke.

Luke:

"You okay?"

Mark is unable to speak and points at the paper-towel holder to Luke's left. Luke passes a handful of towels to Mark.

Mark dries himself off.

"Still pretty out of it."

Luke:

"We should get you home."

Mark nods and smiles weakly at Luke, and the two make their way back to Stephanie. She looks questioningly at Luke.

Luke:

"He'll make it. We just need to go home."

Stephanie nods as she points to an empty bench.

"Wait here. I'm gonna call my mom to pick us up. You guys can get the bikes later."

Stephanie returns in a little while.

"She's on her way."

Luke:

"Let's get our stuff."

They retrieve their backpacks and wait by the curb. Mark is starting to look a bit better. When Stephanie sees her mom's car, she waves her down and they head back to Luke's house.

Stephanie:

"It was a fun day, except for the end."

Mark:

"My sentiments exactly."

Stephanie and her mom drop off Mark and Luke at the front of the house, and they walk through the living room into the kitchen, where Luke's mom and dad and Ricky are having dinner.

Luke's mom:

"Hey, boys. You're home sooner than we expected."

Luke:

"We went on the rides earlier than planned, and Mark got sick from the Giant Dipper."

Luke's mom:

"You okay, honey?"

Mark:

"A lot better, after throwing up."

Luke's mom:

"Why don't you shower and get into clean clothes and then bed. I'll come up in a little while to check on you."

Mark goes upstairs, and Luke joins his family for dinner.

Ricky:

"Things changed from when I saw you guys at the beach."

Luke:

"Except for the end, we had a blast."

Ricky:

"I dug catchin' the waves with my buddies today, except for the one I ate."

Luke's dad:

"Remember guys, we leave for the lake tomorrow."

Luke:

"Oh, that's right."

Luke's dad:

"I want to be on the road by noon. And your mom and I will need everyone's help packing and loading up my truck and the VW."

Luke:

"Okay, Dad."

Ricky:

"Luke, if you guys aren't babies, I'll even take you and Mahte out on the boat skiing."

Luke ignores Ricky's dig.

"That'd be great. Lookin' forward to some early-morning runs on the lake."

Luke's mom:

"Luke, I didn't get a chance to pick the fruits and vegetables for the trip, as your aunt and I lost track of time shopping at the flea market. Can you and Mark give me a hand with that in the morning?"

Luke:

"Sure, Mom."

Luke's mom prepares a tray for Mark of cold ginger ale and hot chicken broth. When she gets to the second floor, she knocks gently on the open bedroom door and peeks inside. She sees her patient lying on his bed.

"I have some things to help settle your stomach."

Mark:

"Thanks, Mrs. Bordet."

Mark sits up, and she places the tray next to him on the bed.

Luke's mom:

"Did the shower help?"

Mark:

"Yes, and it feels good to be in clean clothes."

Luke's mom:

"You rest."

She goes back to the kitchen.

"He seems better."

Luke:

"Thanks, Mom. I'm going up."

She kisses Luke on the cheek.

"Sleep well. We have a busy day tomorrow."

When Luke enters the bedroom, Mark is awake, lying on his side in bed. The empty bowl and glass are on the tray on the dresser.

Luke:

"Hey."

Mark:

"Hey."

Luke:

"I'm gonna grab a shower."

Luke gets clean clothes and goes across the hall into the bathroom.

Mark turns onto his back and, as he stares at the ceiling, thinks about the day: their bike ride to the beach and how empty it was when they first got there. How the frigid ocean water took his breath away when he dove into it. Stephanie and Luke's air hockey contest and quarrel about Luke not spending enough time with her.

Luke comes back, his damp hair combed back and hanging down onto his shoulders. He's in a fresh T-shirt and gym shorts and puts his dirty clothes inside the closet.

Luke:

"Thought you'd be asleep by now."

Mark:

"Just thinking."

Luke pulls back the blanket and top sheet on his bed and climbs in.

"Was quite a day."

Mark:

"Yes, a lot of fun. But one thing is still bothering me."

Luke:

"I thought your stomach was feeling better."

Mark:

"It's fine. I feel bad that I'm the reason you and Stephanie fought."

Luke:

"Yeah, she doesn't like all the time you and I are spending together, but this has happened before. She's also gotten pissed off at me for spending time with other friends."

Mark:

"I could give you guys more space."

Luke:

"No, you won't be here that much longer. Don't worry about it."

Mark:

"I'm starting to feel sunburned."

Luke:

"Me too. We forgot to put on sunblock. I'll be right back."

Luke returns with a clear angular bottle filled with green aloe gel. He sits on his bed and takes off his T-shirt and puts the gel on his arms, stomach, neck and face, careful not to get it in his eyes.

Luke:

"That helps. Here, Mark."

Mark reaches over and takes the bottle from Luke. He takes off his T-shirt and applies the cooling ointment.

Mark:

"I can't reach my upper back. Can you?"

Luke:

"Sure, give me the bottle."

Luke moves from his bed onto Mark's, and Mark turns his back to Luke and closes his eyes as Luke rubs the aloe into his skin.

Luke:

"How's that?"

Mark:

"Much better."

Luke repeats the process on Mark's lower back, after which Mark opens his eyes and turns and smiles at Luke.

Mark:

"Let me do yours."

Luke hands the bottle over and turns his back to Mark, relaxing as Mark massages the gel into his upper back. But when Mark moves his hands to Luke's sides, Luke starts to laugh.

Luke:

"No fair. I'm ticklish there."

Mark:

"Sorry."

But then Mark goes back to the same spot, and Luke laughs and squirms out of Mark's reach.

Luke:

"Hey!"

Mark:

"I couldn't resist."

Mark finishes putting the gel on Luke's back, being careful to avoid his sides this time.

They put their T-shirts back on, and Luke moves back to his bed.

Luke:

"We're leaving for the lake tomorrow and need to help with the packing first thing."

Mark:

"Sure."

Sleep overtakes them, and they fall into a sound rest from the pleasant and eventful day.

Chapter 5

Luke's dad:

"Ricky, let's start by pulling things off the shelves. Then we'll need to wipe them down."

It's 6 a.m. The day has started early for the Bordets, who are getting ready for their annual vacation at San Luis Reservoir, created in the mid-1960s to hold winter and spring runoff for use in irrigating crops.

Luke's dad and Ricky are in the garage getting things out of storage: a big red Coleman cooler with a white lid, fishing poles and a tackle box, Ricky's and Luke's water skis, a tow rope and life jackets, sleeping bags and electric lanterns for sleeping on the houseboat roof at night, and a radio/cassette boom box.

Luke's dad hands the cooler to Ricky.

"Here, take this outside to scrub it inside and out and rinse it off with the garden hose. Use those clean rags to dry it, before you take it to mom in the kitchen."

Ricky takes the cooler and rags out while Luke's dad moves his truck from the garage to the driveway and then returns to pulling things from the shelves and putting them on the backyard grass. Grace, Luke's 23-year-old sister, pulls into the driveway in her beat-up, faded-green VW minibus and parks behind the truck. The van is decorated with flower and peace-sign decals. The side and back windows have open curtains with bright yellow and red flowers.

Grace gets out of the bus, sees her dad working on the lawn, and waves and goes up to him. A free spirit like Janice Joplin, she wears a well-worn beige tank top and jeans with holes in the knees covered by patches sewn on by Luke's mom. Her dad puts down the fishing rods and gear and gives Grace a long hug. It's been a few weeks since they've seen each other.

Grace:

"How ya doing?"

Luke's dad:

"I'm good. You?"

Grace:

"Still waking up. Earlier than what I'm used to."

Luke's dad:

"I'll feel better once the packing is done and we can get on the road."

Grace:

"My stuff is in the back of the VW, but you can move it around to fit other stuff."

Luke's dad:

"Sure, honey."

Grace:

"I'm going to help Mom."

As Grace reaches the back porch, Ricky comes out after having given their mom the cooler. They talk softly.

Ricky:

"Hey, sis."

Grace:

"Hey, bro."

Ricky:

"Ready for a fun drive?"

Grace:

"Got the joints and the tunes."

Ricky:

"Good. Need to chill out. Mom and Dad been getting on my case about paying rent."

Grace:

"Ya may have to up your hours at the auto repair shop."

Ricky:

"Yeah, but that'd cut into my soccer and surfing with the guys."

Grace:

"Life's tough."

Ricky heads back to the garage, and Grace goes into the kitchen, where her mom is kneeling as she packs the cooler with food she has prepared.

Grace:

"Morning, Mom."

Luke's mom gets up from the cooler and hugs her daughter.

"Hi, honey."

Grace:

"How can I help?"

Luke's mom:

"I haven't heard Luke and Mark. Can you go check on them? Have them come down to eat."

Grace walks up to Luke's bedroom and finds the boys awake, lying in bed and talking.

Grace:

"Mom wants you to come down to eat."

Luke:

"Hey, Grace. We just woke up. We'll get started."

Mark:

"Hey, Grace."

Still in their T-shirts and gym shorts, Luke and Mark get out of bed and follow Grace.

Luke:

"Morning, Mom."

Mark:

"Morning, Mrs. Bordet."

Luke's mom:

"Morning, boys. Have some cereal before heading out to the garden to pick stuff for the lake. Make sure you get vegetables for salads and fruit for snacks."

Luke and Mark have cornflakes with milk and drink orange juice.

Luke's mom:

"Do you have enough clean bathing suits, T-shirts and underwear?"

Luke:

"You want us to do laundry too? I think we're fine."

Luke's mom:

"Just check. I don't have time to do it."

Luke sighs.

After breakfast, the boys do their dishes. They get red plastic milk crates from the pantry and go out to the garden.

Luke:

"Mark, you concentrate on the fruit. I'll pick the vegetables."

Once they have filled the crates, they take them inside. Grace is working on loading peanut butter, pancake mix and other nonperishables into cardboard boxes.

"Mom, what else do you need me to pack?"

Luke's mom:

"Look in the pantry for any other items we'll need for breakfasts and lunches."

Luke:

"Let's go check out our clothes."

Mark:

"K."

Back in the bedroom, Luke and Mark open the closet and pull out their laundry baskets, which are full.

Mark:

"Your mom was right to have us check."

Luke:

"Unfortunately. Bring your basket."

The two take their baskets to the first-floor hallway, where the basement door is. Luke opens the door while balancing his basket on his hip.

They walk down into the basement with its gray cement floor. It has the same footprint as the floor above it but without finished walls. The basement is evenly divided by six metal support poles in parallel lines that run the length of the basement, three on each side of the staircase. The year before, Luke had helped his dad spray-paint the poles with dark red Rust-Oleum to keep them from corroding.

The room also is split up by how the family uses it

In the corner under the kitchen, a laundry area has a side-by-side washer and dryer. Above is a shelf that holds laundry detergent, bleach and liquid fabric softener.

A green ping-pong table takes up the space directly beneath the living room. The table has a sagging center net and holds several paddles and balls.

The house's furnace and heating oil tank are located below Luke's parents' bedroom.

And beneath Ricky's bedroom is a storage area lined with floor-to-ceiling wooden shelves that hold canned food and Ball glass jars filled with preserved fruit and pickled vegetables from the garden, along with a storage bin that holds potatoes on one side and apples on the other.

Mark and Luke walk back to the washer and dryer.

Luke:

"Let's sort the clothes into colors and whites."

They pull clothes from the baskets and create two piles on the floor.

Luke opens the washer, and Mark puts the colored clothes into the machine as Luke uses a plastic cup to scoop detergent from the box and sprinkle it onto the clothes. Luke then closes the lid and turns on the machine so it starts filling with hot water.

Mark walks back to the staircase, which is bordered by more wooden shelves that hold boxes with writing in black magic marker that identifies them by occasion: Christmas, Easter, Halloween, birthday.

Mark:

"You guys go all out for the holidays."

Luke:

"My family likes to celebrate, and my dad's an outdoor Christmas lighting buff."

Mark walks over to the ping-pong table.

"Do you play?"

Luke:

"With Ricky or my dad sometimes."

Mark:

"My Uncle Dick, who was married to my Aunt Betty, loved to play. When we went back to Philly in the summer, my sisters and I would play in their basement, sometimes with him. You up for a game while we wait for the wash?"

Luke:

"Sure."

Luke walks to the table and tightens the net so it stands up straight. They go to opposite ends and each pick up a paddle.

Underneath Luke's paddle is a white ping-pong ball, which he hits over to Mark to begin.

The two casually volley for a while.

Luke:

"You ready to start the game?"

Mark:

"Yeah, I'm warmed up."

Luke serves first. As the game proceeds, they realize they're evenly matched and become more aggressive in their play. One wins a point or two, only to be matched by the other. They laugh a lot. The final match point goes to Luke.

Mark:

"Good game."

Luke:

"You let me win."

Mark:

"Nah. You did it fair and square."

Luke notices the washing machine has finished and moves the load of clothes to the dryer while Mark begins the whites in the washer. When they're done, they sit on nearby stools.

Luke's mom comes halfway down the basement steps to check on them.

 "How are you boys making out?"

Luke:

"Our colors are drying, and the whites are in the washer."

Luke's mom:

"Keep at it."

She goes back up to the kitchen, closing the door and leaving Luke and Mark on their own again.

Luke:

"You'll like the lake. It's peaceful. My uncle's houseboat we stay on is connected to five others, and we'll hang out with other kids our age."

Mark:

"Hmm. Cool. You thought any more about smoothing things out with Stephanie?"

Luke:

"She knows I'll be gone for a while. Hopefully, she'll cool down."

Mark:

"Last year, I had a girlfriend on Kwaj, Sharon. Her American dad and Filipino mom met when he was stationed in Manila. Sharon is beautiful."

Luke:

"You guys still dating?"

Mark:

"We did for a few months. We'd go on movie dates."

Luke:

"How'd that go?"

Mark:

"During a movie, we'd make out, not paying too much attention to what was on the screen. Sometimes we'd even go outside to do it. It was fun."

Luke:

"So why'd ya stop?"

Mark:

"I got frustrated because she never wanted to take it any further. So I stopped."

Luke:

"Just like that?"

Mark:

"Well, it wasn't just that. I also realized I was more interested in guys."

Luke:

"Really?"

Mark:

"Yeah, I started looking at my mom's *Playgirl*s when I'd jerk off."

Luke:

"Did you do anything with other guys on Kwaj?"

Mark:

"One time, but I don't think I was ready."

Luke:

"What happened?"

Mark:

"He jerked me off, and I played with him."

Luke:

"Did you like it?"

Mark:

"Yes."

Luke can't bring himself to tell Mark he is having similar feelings for men. They sit in nervous silence until the dryer beeps. Luke puts the dry clothes in a basket and dumps them on the ping-pong table. Mark moves the damp whites to the dryer and turns it on. They each fold their own clothes.

Mark:

"Have you and Stephanie had sex?"

Luke:

"We've made out a lot."

Mark:

"Nothing else?"

Luke:

"Not yet."

Mark feels Luke's reluctance to talk more and stops pushing.

As Mark and Luke wait for the whites to dry, they casually hit the ping-pong ball back and forth. When the dryer is done, they fold the rest, put their clothes in their baskets and walk upstairs to the kitchen. They see Luke's mom and sister about to take the packed food out back.

Luke:

"Mom, we're done."

Luke's mom:

"Pack and then take it out to load."

Luke's mom and Grace carry the full cooler and boxes outside for Luke's dad and Ricky to load into the truck and minibus.

After all the food is out at the vehicles, Luke's mom and Grace sit at the kitchen table for a coffee break.

Grace:

"What do you think of me taking Luke and Mark on a road trip?"

Luke's mom:

"To where?"

Grace:

"L.A., to Magic Mountain. I think it would be something fun for the three of us to do."

Luke's mom:

"How long would it take?"

Grace:

"About three days, one to drive down, one at the amusement park, and one to get back."

Luke's mom:

"Hmm."

Grace:

"So?"

Luke's mom:

"I think they'd enjoy it. First, use the drive up to the lake as a test run."

Grace:

"Ricky and I were going to ride on our own to the lake, but I prefer your idea."

Luke's mom:

"Ricky will ride in the truck with Dad and me."

Grace:

"He's not going to be happy about that."

Luke's mom:

"We'll see."

Luke's dad and Ricky also are talking about the drive.

Luke's dad:

"Ricky, I want you to ride with me and Mom. The boys will go with Grace."

Ricky:

"No, Grace and I plan to ride together in her VW. Luke and Mark can go with you."

Luke's dad knows Ricky's motives but plans to use the drive to talk with his son about behaving more like an adult.

Luke's dad:

"There is only room in the front of my truck for three."

Ricky:

"The boys can squeeze in between you and Mom."

Luke's dad:

"No. You're going to ride with me and Mom."

Ricky explodes:

"You can't force me! I'm going by myself on my motorcycle!"

Ricky storms off to the back alley behind the garage.

Realizing Ricky needs to blow off steam, Luke's father lets him go and finishes loading things up.

Meanwhile in the kitchen, Luke's mom and Grace have finished their break and are making lunch for the family to eat before the drive.

Luke's dad finishes loading the truck and covers the bed with a blue plastic tarp, securing everything with a rope that he zig-zags over the tarp and connects to hooks along the sides of the truck bed. Pleased with the results, he heads back inside.

Luke's dad:

"Hi, Mom. We're ready to go."

Luke's mom:

"Okay, dear. Sit down and eat."

Luke's mom and Grace bring the sandwiches they have prepared along with bags of potato chips and drinks to the table. The three begin eating and are joined by Mark and Luke, who have packed their things in Grace's VW.

As they are eating, Ricky has prepared for making the trip on his motorcycle. He joins the group in the kitchen.

Luke's mom:

"There are two more sandwiches left and some chips. Why don't you sit down and eat."

Ricky is still in a foul mood:

"Yeah, sure."

Luke's dad:

"So it's settled. Mom and I are going in the truck, Luke and Mark will ride with Grace, and Ricky's taking his bike."

As he eats, Ricky grunts to acknowledge what his father has said. The others throw out their trash, and Grace and Luke's mom clean up.

Ricky:

"Meet you guys at the houseboat. I need time to finish packing."

Luke's dad:

"Make sure to lock up the house and garage before leaving."

Ricky doesn't respond.

Luke's dad:

"Okay?"

Ricky:

"Yeah, I'll do it."

The rest of the group walk out to the two vehicles. Grace pulls her minibus onto the grass and turns it around so it's facing the street, while Luke's dad moves the truck on the driveway closer to the street and rolls down his window:

"You follow me."

Grace:

"Okay, Dad."

The two vehicles turn left at the end of the driveway and take the entrance onto the highway for the two-hour drive to the lake, which goes smoothly, with one bathroom break at a highway rest stop.

They arrive in the late afternoon, park in the lot next to the lake and get out and stretch.

Luke's dad:

"Luke, why don't you and Mark walk with me. We need to go farther down to get your uncle's attention on the houseboat, so he can drive the powerboat to the parking lot and help us take everything over."

A short while later, the three return to the parking lot, and Luke's uncle drives across the lake to get them. The next hour and a half is spent ferrying people and belongings between the lot and the houseboat, with Ricky arriving during that time. The new arrivals are greeted by family members already aboard, and as twilight turns to night, they settle down, the adults in their beds on the inside first level and the teenagers and young adults on the uncovered top deck, falling asleep in sleeping bags under the stars.

Chapter 6

The six houseboats anchored together in the cove are like a small floating town in a predawn mist. All is quiet, except for the crickets. The motor boat is tied alongside Luke's uncle's houseboat, and the group on its roof deck are still asleep.

Mark stirs in his sleeping bag and opens his eyes. He gets out, grabs his rolled-up bath towel and bathing suit, and makes his way in between Luke and the others, careful not to step on anyone.

He climbs down an outside ladder to the first level and goes inside to a cramped bathroom, with a shower stall, sink and toilet, and closes the door. A clear plastic shower curtain painted with an ocean motif hangs on the front of the stall. Mark puts his towel and bathing suit on the toilet tank and starts the shower, testing the water before taking off his clothes and getting in.

As he finishes waking up, he leans forward and lets the water cascade over his head and body.

He soaps up and begins to play with himself, the pleasure apparent in his face.

Mark is startled by the bathroom door opening. Luke enters carrying a towel, bathing suit and toothbrush. Luke's long hair falls in his eyes, and Mark stops what he's doing.

Luke:

"Morning. I didn't hear you get up. I need to brush my teeth."

Mark:

"Yeah, I just woke up and was trying not to disturb anyone."

Luke puts toothpaste on his toothbrush and begins brushing, pushing his hair out of his eyes so he can see clearly see himself in the small mirror above the sink.

Mark turns off the shower water, opens the curtain and looks at Luke:

"Can you hand me my towel and bathing suit?"

Luke tosses Mark's bathing suit and rolled-up towel to him, looking at Mark as he does. Midair the towel straightens out and Mark's toothbrush falls to the floor. Mark catches the towel and bathing suit.

Luke picks up Mark's toothbrush and places it on the sink.

Mark:

"Thanks."

Luke gives Mark a "you're welcome" smile, and Mark dries off his body. He puts on his bathing suit, stands next to Luke and brushes his teeth at the sink. Due to room's small size, their shoulders and arms touch as they brush their teeth.

Luke takes off his T-shirt, sweatpants and boxers and puts on his bathing suit, and they quietly walk out to the motor boat.

Ricky is in the driver's seat starting the engine.

Ricky:

"Luke, get the rope."

Luke unties the boat from the houseboat and looks at Mark, who is by the outboard engine tying the tow rope to the end of the boat.

Ricky steers the boat slowly out of the cove. The boat picks up speed as it enters an open expanse of water surrounded by golden grassy hills with the sun breaking over them. The haze lifts, revealing a bright morning. The glasslike water snakes through the hills. When the boat reaches the center of the lake, Ricky stops it.

Ricky:

"Who wants to go first?"

Mark looks at Luke, who shakes his head.

Mark:

"Me."

Mark throws the tow rope, life jacket and ski into the water and dives in. When his head emerges, Mark shivers from the cold early-morning water and takes a deep breath. He puts on the life jacket and positions the ski in front of him, securing his feet in the ski's footholds. He grabs the tow-rope handle tightly. As the boat again gathers speed, the rope pulls taut. The water pushes against Mark's body until he fully comes out on top of it. The wind whips against his face as he looks at the sunburnt hills gliding past him and hears the rattlesnakes in the distance.

Luke gives Mark a thumbs–up, and Mark smiles back.

After several minutes of skiing, Mark loses his balance, drops the rope and dives into the water. He pushes the floating ski in front of him while swimming back to the boat, climbs into the boat and takes off his life jacket. He is breathing deeply.

Luke:

"Nice run."

Mark:

"Thanks. I was a bit shaky at first, but enjoyed it once I got the hang of being on one ski."

Ricky:

"Mahte did it."

Mark glares at Ricky.

Luke's and Mark's hands touch as Mark gives the life jacket to Luke. Luke puts on the life jacket and jumps into the water. When he comes up, he shakes the water off his hair and out of his eyes.

Luke secures the ski and tow rope in front of him and gives Ricky a thumbs-up. Ricky guns the engine and Luke pops up on top of the water. He expertly maneuvers the ski back and forth across the boat's wake until his arms tire, and he intentionally lets go of the rope and sinks back into the water.

Mark:

"He's down."

Ricky looks back, sees Luke in the water and circles the boat back to him and stops. Luke hands the ski to Mark, who places it on the boat floor and assists Luke as he climbs back in.

Mark:

"You were really good out there."

Luke:

"Thanks. I've had a lot of practice."

Ricky:

"We're going to head back."

Mark and Luke secure everything. Ricky drives back to the cove, slows the boat as it comes alongside the houseboat and kills the engine. Luke jumps over to the houseboat, and Mark throws the docking rope to Luke, who ties it to a large hook.

Mark and Ricky join Luke back on the houseboat, and they walk inside, where the others are awake, talking and enjoying scrambled eggs, pancakes and coffee. The three make plates for themselves, with Luke spreading peanut butter on his pancakes before pouring on syrup.

Mark:

"I've never heard of peanut butter on pancakes."

Luke:

"It tastes really good."

Mark tries the combination and finds that he likes it.

Luke:

"The lake was perfect for skiing this morning."

Ricky:

"Yeah, even Mahte was able to get up on a single ski."

As the day progresses, the young people jump and dive off the houseboats and swim in the water. They splash each other and laugh, float in inner tubes, drink sodas and eat potato chips and pretzels while listening to Top 40 music on the boom box. They sunbathe under the warm California sky.

Throughout the late morning and early afternoon, Luke and Mark talk, joke and enjoy each other's company.

Midafternoon, the two decide to take a walk.

Luke:

"Mom, Mark and I are going on shore."

Luke's mom:

"Okay, honey, be careful."

Mark and Luke swim to shore and start walking until they are out of view of the others. They are in their bathing suits and walk gingerly on the dirt and rocks, which are hard on their bare feet.

They stop to have a friendly rock-skipping contest.

As they begin to walk again, the boys move a bit inland and the low-lying trees and brush become thicker. Luke leads the way with Mark following close behind, admiring Luke's tan back and legs.

They come to a small clearing of grass, on the opposite edge of which is an adult mountain lion in a crouched position. Luke spots the lion first, stops and signals Mark to stop. The mountain lion maintains her position and begins hissing and growling. Mark stays still while Luke yells and picks up sticks and rocks from the ground and throws them at the mountain lion until it turns and runs away from them.

Luke touches Mark's shoulder, and Mark reaches up his hand to cover Luke's.

Luke:

"You okay?"

Mark:

"I was scared but now am relieved. How did you know what to do?"

Luke:

"Ricky has hiked here and knows about the mountain lions. He told me what to do if I ever ran into one."

They both take deep breaths and relax. They look at each other for a minute longer, drop their hands to their sides and move into the center of the clearing. They sit close together in the secluded spot.

Mark:

"I had no idea what to do. I'm glad you knew."

Mark reaches out and hugs Luke in thanks.

Luke:

"Me too."

They sit peacefully, enjoying the sun, breeze and midday sound of birds. After a while, they both lay back and Luke starts a tickling and wrestling match, and Mark responds playfully. They laugh and try to overpower each other. Luke straddles Mark, who is on his back and lies still. Luke gently touches Mark's bare chest and underarms, and Mark closes his eyes. After several minutes, they reverse positions, and with his hands Mark explores Luke's chest and nipples.

After a while, they both return to lying on their backs and watch clouds float by. The sun now is at a lower angle, and its light takes on a darker glow.

Luke:

"We should get back. It looks like it's getting close to dinner."

Mark:

"Good. I'm hungry."

Mark and Luke retrace their steps back to where they got out of the lake, dive into the water and swim back to the houseboats. The group is eating hamburgers, hot dogs, corn on the cob and potato salad, and the adults are drinking beer.

Luke looks for and finds Ricky sitting on the top deck with a cluster of teenagers, talking and smoking cigarettes.

Luke:

"We ran into a mountain lion on shore. I did what you told me and scared it off."

Ricky:

"I'm happy it worked."

Later that night, all the young adults are on an open upper deck, sitting or lying on top of their sleeping bags. The sky is a black-blue canopy, sprinkled with bright pinpoints of stars. They are talking, laughing and passing around a joint.

Mark and Luke lay next to each other.

Mark:

"Good night, Luke."

Luke:

"Night, man."

As they gaze up at the stars, they fall off to sleep, looking

forward to another day together.

Chapter 7

The road trip to Magic Mountain theme park outside of Los Angeles begins with Grace picking up Luke and Mark at the Bordet house. She is dressed in her usual tank top and patched-up jeans and pulls her VW into the driveway and parks in front of the garage. She jumps out of the van, takes the back steps two at a time and goes inside. No one is up, and she quietly goes through the kitchen and upstairs to Luke's bedroom. The door is shut, so she knocks softly, waits a minute and, hearing no response, goes inside. Luke and Mark are asleep, Luke on his side turned to the wall and Mark on his back snoring like a freight train.

On the floor by the two dormer windows sit Mark's packed suitcase and backpack, Luke's large red duffel bag full of clothes, and two rolled-up sleeping bags, with pillows stacked on top of them.

Grace talks in a loud whisper:

"Hey, guys. Up and at 'em. We need to hit the road so we can be in L.A. tonight."

Excited about the trip, Luke and Mark wake up right away and kick the covers off. Mark has a morning hard-on and adjusts it quickly in his shorts. Grace sees Mark's attempt to hide it but doesn't say anything. Luke and Mark get out of bed, focused on getting ready to leave. Grace picks up the pillows and sleeping bags on the floor and grabs the pillows from the beds, still warm from Luke's and Mark's heads.

Grace:

"I'm gonna take this stuff down to my van while you guys finish getting ready. Then bring the rest of your stuff down."

The boys change into their road-trip shorts and T-shirts, as well as flip-flops they can easily kick off in the VW. They are now comfortable with getting undressed in front of one another and go into the bathroom together to take turns brushing their teeth at the sink and peeing.

Once done, Mark and Luke get their belongings and carry them downstairs.

Luke:

"Go ahead out. I'll be right there."

Mark takes his luggage out back as Luke writes a quick note to his mom and dad, places it on the refrigerator under the magnet and goes out to Grace's van.

Grace is in the van making space for the boys' things.

"Give me a sec, okay?"

Mark and Luke hand their bags to her, and she secures them and climbs out.

Grace:

"Let's do this! Luke, you're going to ride shotgun to start. Mark, why don't you sit behind him."

Luke and Mark get in, and Grace climbs up into the driver's seat.

There is a big box of music cassette tapes on the floor next to the driver's seat. Grace looks in the box and pulls out a tape and pushes it into the cassette player in the center of the van's dashboard. The three sing along until the song's conclusion, laughing at the end.

For the first half of the trip, Grace takes Route 1 because of its scenic views of the Pacific as the road hugs the Central California coastline. The three admire Monterey Bay during the first leg of the drive, enjoying the sights of Monterey and Carmel-by-the-Sea.

Grace:

"Luke, I'm gonna have you be in charge of the music for a while."

Luke puts the music box on his lap, flips through the cassettes and takes out four, and returns the box next to Grace's feet.

As the van enters the coastal part of Big Sur, Luke puts the next tape into the player. The music further relaxes the three, as they take in the deep blue color of the Pacific on Luke's side and the pine-tree-covered mountains on Grace's.

A while later, Grace asks:

"I'm getting hungry. How about you guys?"

The question pulls Luke and Mark out of their daydreaming, and they both nod at her.

Grace notices a series of roadside signs announcing a diner ahead.

"I know where we'll stop."

A few minutes later she pulls the van into a dirt parking lot filled with cars and trucks. Grace, Luke and Mark go inside. They see a waitress standing behind the counter that runs the length of the diner. "Phyllis" is on her name tag on the left-breast pocket of her pink-and-white uniform, and she is taking the order of a customer sitting at the counter. She looks up from her order pad and directs the trio to sit at the window booth next to the front door. They slide into the booth, pull out the menus propped up on their table and peruse the contents.

Phyllis finishes taking the customer's order, attaching it to the circular metal order rack for the short-order cook working at the grill. She comes over to their booth and takes the pen from behind her ear.

"What can I get you folks?"

Grace:

"I'll have the cheeseburger and fries, with a Coke."

Luke:

"Can you give me the same, but with a vanilla shake?"

Mark:

"I'll have the same as him."

After scribbling down the three orders, Phyllis goes back and adds them to the rack.

Phyllis brings out their food and drinks a few minutes later, and the three eat. As Grace and Mark finish their meals, Luke heads to the men's room in the back. As he enters, he sees the bathroom has two stalls off to his left and three urinals to his right. He uses the urinal closest to him, and then washes his hands and returns to the table.

Grace is at the counter paying the bill.

"Let's go, guys."

Back on the road, Grace looks at the dashboard clock and sees they are behind schedule. She directs the van inland to Interstate 5 and speeds up, getting them to Los Angeles near the theme park by midevening.

Grace:

"I'm going to try and save us some money and find a place where we can park and sleep in the van for the night."

She sees a large supermarket parking lot and drives the van to the end farthest from the store. The three pull shut the curtains on the VW's windows.

Luke and Mark unroll their sleeping bags in the back of the van, climb into them and fall asleep quickly. Grace lies down across the bench seat in the middle and soon is sleeping as well.

Two hours later, at 10 p.m., the three are awakened by a sharp rapping on the driver's window. A tall California state trooper with a crew cut and a large flashlight peers into the van. Grace climbs in front on the driver's side and rolls down the window. She groggily looks at the police officer.

"License and registration please, ma'am."

Grace reaches in the glove compartment and hands them to him.

State trooper:

"Who's in the car with you?"

Grace:

"My brother and his friend."

Trooper:

"Ma'am, you can't be parked here overnight. You're going to have to move your van."

Grace:

"Yes, sir. We'll get out of here."

Luke and Mark watch the interaction from their sleeping bags.

Grace starts the van, pulls out of the parking lot and drives on the road for a while, until finding a cheap motel.

Grace turns the van into the motel entrance and parks next to the small lobby, which is enclosed in glass, revealing a high blue counter behind which sits a 20-something nighttime clerk with disheveled brown hair and at least a three-day-old stubble. He is almost falling asleep as he reads a tattered copy of *Carrie*, Stephen King's novel about a girl with telekinetic powers and her abusive mother.

As Grace gets out of the van, she turns her head to the boys.

"You guys wait here."

She goes into the lobby. While signing the ledger, she sees a bowl filled with books of matches advertising the motel. She takes some and puts them in her right jeans pocket as she finishes checking in. A short time later, the three are walking toward their room with their luggage. As they go farther back on the property, Grace notices the motel has an in-ground pool.

They go to their room, and Grace unlocks the door. The room's walls have green-and-yellow-striped wallpaper that has seen better days. The room's two queen-size beds are made and have bedspreads that complement the wallpaper, both in color and condition.

Grace puts down her bag on the bed closest to the door.

"I'll use this bed, and you guys can take the other one."

Luke and Mark put their things on top of the large dresser across from their bed and flop down on the bed side by side, discovering the mattress sags in the middle.

The room has a picture window that occupies the entire front wall, except for the outside door. The window's heavy privacy curtains are open. Grace turns and looks out the window at the pool, which is only two doors down from their room.

Grace:

"Ya wanna take a dip?"

Luke:

"Sure!"

Grace:

"Let's do it."

Grace goes into the bathroom and comes out with three large white bath towels. She hands one to each of them, puts the room key in her pocket and goes out.

Luke:

"Aren't you putting on a suit?"

Grace:

"Nah, it's late. No one else is around. Gonna go commando. See ya guys out there."

Mark:

"Shouldn't we wear bathing suits?"

Luke looks at Mark, shrugs his shoulders and holds out his palms.

They walk out of the room with their clothes on, carrying their towels. Mark closes the door tightly behind him.

When Luke and Mark reach the pool, Grace's clothes are already in a pile on one of the white plastic chairs, and she is swimming in the deep end, her naked butt in clear view in the well-lit blue water. The boys stand for a few minutes, watching Grace do leisurely circles in the water, as they build their courage to join her. They look around to see if anyone is watching and strip down to their birthday suits, jumping into the deep end with abandon.

The three swim around for another half an hour or so, at the end of which Grace is still in the deep end, and Luke and Mark are in the shallow end splashing each other. Grace gets out using the ladder. She walks over to the chair that has her clothes on it and gets dressed. Mark and Luke's horseplay intensifies, and Mark throws Luke toward the deep end and follows him.

Grace sits on her chair and watches them. She reaches into her left pocket and pulls out half a joint she and Ricky had smoked at the lake. She reaches into her right pocket for the motel matches, lights up the doobie and inhales deeply, leaning back and waiting for the familiar calm to settle in. Mark and Luke are in the deep end with their arms and shoulders resting on the cement deck while their bodies hang down in the water. They periodically bring their bodies up horizontally by kicking the water as they remain in place.

Mark:

"I'm glad I got the nerve to come in without a bathing suit. The water feels good on my naked body."

Luke:

"It's a great way to end the first day of our road trip."

Mark:

"I think tomorrow at Magic Mountain is going to be really fun."

Luke:

"Definitely."

Mark:

"But I'm starting to think about having to go back to Kwaj in three days."

Luke:

"Mark, don't mess things up."

Mark:

"How can you say that?"

Luke:

"It is what it is."

Mark:

"It's not fair. We're just getting to really know each other again."

Luke:

"We can still write."

Mark can feel the frustration rise. He knows that once he's back on Kwaj the two won't be able to talk like this anymore, as long-distance phone calls between Kwaj and the U.S. use a radio phone service, which only allows for short, barely understandable conversations, with each caller having to say "over" each time they finish speaking — as if they were using walkie-talkies.

Mark thinks about how their past communications have consisted of long, detailed letters from him to Luke, with Luke responding on postcards with pictures of Santa Cruz on one side and a few sentences from Luke on the other. Those postcards are what motivated Mark to ask his parents if he could go to Santa Cruz to visit Luke. But the cards' brevity is what now makes Mark lash out.

"Yeah, and with the way you write, I'll pretty much be having a one-sided conversation with myself!"

Luke:

"Whoa, dude! Where's this comin' from?"

Mark:

"I know once I'm back on the island, we won't be able to

talk like this."

Luke:

"So maybe I can ask my parents if you can come back next

summer."

Mark:

"But that's a long time to wait, for us to be able to talk

again."

Luke:

"I can't change that."

Mark:

"It sucks!"

Luke:

"Yeah."

Mark begins to cry, first almost imperceptibly and then in big, loud, gulping sobs.

Luke:

"C'mon. Let's get out."

Mark continues to cry, but not as forcefully, and the two raise themselves on their arms, placing their feet on the pool deck and standing up. They walk over to the chairs where they have left their clothes, get dressed and sit. Grace is asleep in her chair, the full effect of the long drive and the weed having knocked her out.

Luke looks at the water in the pool, giving Mark time to let the rest of his cries out. After a few minutes, Mark has calmed down, and Luke smiles gently and places his hand on Mark's shoulder.

Mark lets out a long sigh and shakes his head back and forth.

Luke:

"I will try to send you longer responses."

This causes Mark to let out one of his signature hearty laughs, and it's Mark's own laughter that helps calm him.

Mark:

"You won't. But I appreciate you saying it."

Mark's laughter also awakens Grace from her pot-induced slumber.

Grace:

"Okay, guys, we need to hit the hay. We have a big day tomorrow at the park."

The three walk the short distance back to their room, with Grace unlocking the door and falling into her bed on top of the covers. She almost immediately is back asleep. Luke and Mark walk over to their bed and pull back the cover and top sheet, getting in and pulling only the top sheet back over their bodies. The sagginess of the bed causes their sides to touch.

Luke:

"Things will look better tomorrow. We're going to have a blast at the park."

Luke looks over at Mark when he doesn't respond and sees that he has fallen asleep. Luke closes his eyes and joins Mark and Grace in dreamland.

Chapter 8

Grace smiles broadly as the strong wind blows her hair back off her shoulders and echoes in her ears. She hears the roar of the boat's engine at full throttle and grips the steering wheel tightly to keep the boat on a straight path. Grace is standing and in her legs and feet feels the bucking of the boat, like a 2,000-pound bull in a rodeo, as it skips across the choppy waves being kicked up by the South Pacific trade winds. She feels the intense midday sun on her already dark skin, and the air is heavy with humidity from the ocean.

Grace's best friend, Cindy, sits to her left and is wearing a polka-dot bikini. Her long, sun-bleached hair is blowing around, sometimes covering her face. Luke and Mark are at the front of the boat, flat on their stomachs. They have bathing suits and red life jackets on and are holding on for dear life enjoying the ride.

The boat arrives at the quarter-mile-long, flat, palm-tree-covered island, and Grace slows it to a stop.

Grace:

"Cindy, throw the anchor over the side."

Grace slowly drives the boat forward and lodges the anchor in the coral head beneath them.

They will spend the next several hours at the island, where Luke and Mark will snorkel to look at a colorful array of fish, and Grace and Cindy will wander topless, searching for seashells and Japanese glass fishing floats that have washed ashore.

Hearing the noisy caws of seagulls above her, Grace turns her face upward, looking directly into the sun, momentarily blinded. She blinks rapidly and shields her eyes with her right hand.

The Southern California sunrise, streaming through the motel room's picture window, brings Grace out of her recurring dream about a Kwaj boat trip the four of them had taken. They had gone for the day on a white Boston Whaler to one of the small uninhabited islands within the atoll's 839-square-mile lagoon — the world's largest.

Grace looks at the alarm clock. Its large red digital numbers read 6:22.

Mark:

"Morning, Grace."

Grace looks over at Mark, who is lying in bed awake.

Grace:

"Morning."

Mark:

"I noticed you were tossing and turning."

Grace:

"I had an intense dream."

Mark:

"About what?"

Grace:

"One of the Kwaj boat trips I took you, Cindy and Luke on."

Mark:

"Are you serious?"

Grace:

"I've had the dream before. It's one of my favorite Kwaj memories."

Mark:

"I had the same dream last night."

The two look at each other in disbelief.

Grace:

"I'm getting goosebumps."

Mark:

"This is too weird."

They lay perplexed, looking at each other and shaking their

heads.

Mark:

"Don't we need to start getting ready?"

Grace:

"We do."

Mark gently shakes Luke's shoulder, waking him out of his own dream.

Mark:

"Morning."

Luke:

"Hey."

Mark:

"You're not going to believe this … Grace and I had the same dream last night."

Luke:

"What about?"

Grace:

"One of our Kwaj boat trips with Cindy."

Luke:

"Ha ha ha. You guys are jokin', right?"

Grace:

"No. Why do you say that?"

Luke:

"Because this isn't the first time, Grace, you've taken advantage of my gullibility."

Grace:

"Honestly, we're not pulling a prank."

Luke realizes Grace and Mark are serious.

Luke:

"Well, you're not going to believe me either."

Grace:

"Why?"

Luke:

"I just had the same dream."

The three look at each other in bewilderment.

Grace begins humming the theme song to *The Twilight Zone*.

Luke:

"How do we explain it?"

Grace:

"We don't. We just get started."

Grace swings her legs out of bed, goes to the enclosed section of the bathroom with the toilet and shower, and closes the door to pee. After she comes out, she stops at the vanity with a sink and large mirror and brushes her teeth and hair. Luke and Mark also get ready.

Grace:

"First, we're gonna head over to the grocery store from last night. Because we got a motel room, we need to save money by getting today's food there instead of in the park. Make sure we also get ice for the cooler to keep things cold."

Grace drives to the supermarket, and they buy what they need. Once back at the minibus, they store their purchases in the cooler and in the van's cabinets.

Grace:

"Let's eat breakfast here before heading over to Magic Mountain. Can you guys get the stuff ready?"

Luke:

"Sure."

Luke and Mark get out blueberry muffins, yogurt and bottles of orange juice while Grace maps out how to get to the park. They eat breakfast standing next to the minibus. Mark deposits the trash in a nearby dumpster, and they head over to the park.

When they arrive, the parking lot is already half full. The park will be crowded today. A line of parking attendants direct cars into open spaces. As Grace follows the line, she sees each parking section is designated with a sign on top of a light pole with a park mascot name, such as "King Blop," "Bleep" or "Bloop," to help visitors find their vehicles later. Grace pulls into a spot in "The Wizard" section.

They walk for five minutes to the entrance, where eight ticket kiosks guard against nonpaying intruders. Each wooden kiosk is painted green and has a large sliding window. A teenage sales clerk takes their money, helps them put on blue wristbands and gives them park maps. They spot their first ride, Revolution, North America's first steel roller coaster with a vertical loop. For 25 minutes, they snake their way to the front of the line.

Grace:

"Finally!"

Once snug in their seats, they creep upward at a 45-degree angle until reaching the ride's initial crest. They first descent is quick, followed by a series of fast peaks, dips and sideways curves. The car climbs another large hill and plunges them into the vertical loop.

Luke:

"Woo-hoo!"

They hold their arms up to intensify the feeling of being upside down. They hit a few more peaks and tight curves before coming to a stop where they started.

Mark:

"That was definitely worth the wait."

The three exit, walk to a shaded area with benches and sit to look at the map.

Mark:

"I need to pee. Be right back."

Grace uses this opportunity to talk with Luke privately:

"You know you can talk with me about anything, right?"

Luke is unsure where his sister is going.

Grace:

"Like if you're having an issue with Stephanie that you don't feel comfortable discussing with Mom and Dad."

Earlier that week while getting ready for the lake, Grace had gone partway down the basement steps for canned food when she overheard Mark talking with Luke about his sexuality. From Luke's questions, she sensed Luke may be interested in men too and wanted her brother to know he could safely talk with her.

Luke:

"If I need to, I'll let you know."

Luke changes the subject:

"Look. We're not too far from the Log Jammer. Let's go on that."

Grace:

"Sure."

Mark returns, and they make their way to the Log Jammer log flume water ride, which has a long line. The boys wait patiently while Grace gets antsy. They finally make it to the front of the line.

The ride begins with their log floating through several gentle curves. A black conveyer belt then catches the log, taking it up a steep hill through a tunnel of trees. At the tunnel's end, the log plops back into the next water chute. It bumps to the right and left as it moves through the curves and builds speed. After a minute, they are deposited on a second black conveyor, which carries them upward where they have a clear view of the bright blue sky. They then reach the ride's two steep watery drops, the first of which lasts a few seconds, half as long as the second. Luke and Mark scream as their log splashes into the final pool, throwing water into the log and soaking them.

On the exit platform, Luke, Mark and Grace inspect their drenched clothes.

Grace:

"These aren't going to dry anytime soon."

Mark:

"I'm getting hungry."

Grace:

"Let's go back to the VW to get changed and eat."

They make their way back to the parking area, now full of cars, trucks and RVs, to find their minibus. Grace gets in to turn on the vehicle and air conditioning, hoping to get rid of enough heat so they can comfortably eat inside. Climbing into the center of the vehicle, she unlocks the sliding side door and opens a narrow tall cabinet on her left, pulling out their towels and dry clothes. They change standing next to the van, climbing in when they need privacy.

Once changed, they get into the minibus' center area, which has two padded benches facing each other. The bench closest to the driver's seat fits one person and has a small metal sink and square linoleum-covered serving table next to it. The other bench runs almost the full width of the minivan and seats up to three people. Grace climbs onto the front bench, and Luke and Mark sit on the other one. Between the benches is a Murphy table, which Grace pulls down into its horizontal position.

She opens the cooler on the floor, takes out sliced ham and cheese, lettuce, mayo, orange soda and apples and places them on the table. From a storage cabinet, Luke gets disposable plates and utensils, bread and potato chips. The three make their sandwiches and eat.

Mark:

"So far, I liked the roller coaster the best. My stomach didn't even mind it."

Luke:

"Yeah, Mark, we don't want a repeat of the boardwalk incident."

The two laugh. Grace looks perplexed but doesn't probe.

Luke:

"I wanna go on the Sky Tower next. It'll give us a bird's-eye view of the park. Maybe even L.A."

Grace:

"I'm game, as long as it doesn't have another long line."

The three finish lunch, put the leftovers away and clean up.

They go back in the park and walk to the Sky Tower, where a line even longer than the first two awaits.

Grace:

"Not again!"

Luke and Mark look at her pleadingly. Grace holds up her right hand to them and thinks for a minute.

Grace:

"Here's what we're gonna do."

Luke and Mark look at her hopefully.

Grace:

"You guys do this one on your own. I'm going to pee. I'll be waiting at the exit when you're done."

Grace heads to the restroom as the boys get in line. They wait more than 40 minutes before getting in the Sky

Tower's elevator. At the top, they have great views of the park and the surrounding area of Valencia, including low-lying mountains in the distance. As Mark looks at those mountains, a bright pinpoint of light shines in his eyes for several seconds. He blinks and the light is gone.

Mark:

"Luke, did you see that light in the mountains?"

Luke:

"What light?"

Mark:

"It was right over there."

Luke:

"I didn't see it."

Mark:

"Maybe it was the sun reflecting off the water."

Luke:

"Maybe."

Mark shrugs and forgets about it, and they enjoy the view some more. Once satisfied, they take the elevator down to look for Grace. They're surprised when she's not at the exit.

Luke:

"Mark, you wait here, in case she comes back."

Mark:

"Okay."

Luke:

"I'm gonna look for her while walking."

Mark keeps scanning the crowd. After Luke returns with only a frown, they wait on an exit bench.

Mark:

"Where do you think she is?"

Luke:

"She might have gone back to the van."

After another hour without any sign of Grace, Mark gets up and stops a park employee walking by.

"Hi, sir. My friend and I got separated from his older sister. Can an announcement be made on the PA system to help us find her?"

The employee points to his left.

"You see that two-story building with windows on the top floor?"

Mark:

"Yes."

Park employee:

"That's our main office. Go and ask for the assistant park manager. She may be able to help."

Mark:

"Thanks."

Mark and Luke go and explain their predicament to the assistant park manager. She is in her early 40s, with a short blonde perm and a green blazer.

Assistant park manager:

"I'll announce it. Wait here."

She has them sit in a first-floor waiting area and returns shortly.

Assistant park manager:

"I announced it several times. Now we have to wait for your sister."

While Mark and Luke enjoyed the Sky Tower and were looking for Grace, she had her own adventure. After using the restroom, she was on her way back to get the boys when a cute stoner with long brown hair and beard began walking next to her. Charlie was a head taller, about her age and dressed in well-worn jeans and a black Grateful Dead T-shirt.

Charlie:

"Hey, you."

Grace:

"Hey."

Charlie:

"How's it goin'?"

Grace:

"I'm going to get my younger brother and his friend."

Charlie:

"I'm Charlie."

Grace:

"Grace."

Charlie:

"I'm with some of my buddies, but we split up for a while."

Grace:

"Have fun. I need to get back to the Sky Tower so I'm there when they get out."

Charlie:

"Okay if I walk with you?"

Grace:

"Sure. Why not?"

Charlie points at his T-shirt:

"Ever been to a Dead concert?"

Grace:

"Not yet, but want to."

Charlie:

"I'm a Dead head. So far this summer, my buddies and me have seen them in San Diego and L.A., hangin' out, gettin' high, groovin' to their music."

Grace:

"You have a joint?"

Charlie:

"Yeah. Wanna partake?"

Grace calculates how long she has before she needs to get Luke and Mark.

"Sure. But only for a little. How 'bout we go back to my VW?"

The newly united pair make a U-turn and head back to the minibus, where Grace unlocks the side door and they climb in.

Charlie:

"Nice ride!"

Grace turns on the VW and puts in a tape with the volume down.

Grace:

"It's a bit run-down but gets me where I need to go."

Charlie pulls out a joint and a yellow Bic lighter.

They sit on the wide middle bench. Charlie lights up and they each take a drag.

Grace leans her head on the seat back.

Grace:

"Good stuff."

Charlie:

"Yeah."

The two relax into their high, listen to the music and turn toward each other.

Grace:

"This is nice."

Charlie kisses Grace, first softly, and when she positively responds, with more passion. They slide into a horizontal position, with Grace on top, and continue making out until

Grace's hazy brain half hears the assistant park manager on the PA:

"Grace Bordet. Please come to the office near the Sky Tower to meet your brother."

Grace jumps off of Charlie.

"Oh, shit!"

Charlie:

"What?"

She quickly opens the sliding door and steps into the parking lot, as the announcement repeats:

"Grace Bordet. Please come to the office near the Sky Tower to meet your brother."

Charlie is out of the van as well, and Grace locks it.

Grace:

"I gotta go."

Charlie:

"What about …"

Grace doesn't hear the rest as she runs to the office, which she enters out of breath.

Luke:

"Thank God!"

Grace:

"You guys! I'm so sorry."

She hugs Luke and then Mark.

Grace:

"I got sidetracked. Thought I'd be back before you came out."

Luke:

"We're just glad we found you."

The assistant manager comes back downstairs.

"I see you guys found each other."

Grace:

"Thank you so much."

While walking out, the three suddenly realize how tired they are. The day's excitement has drained their energy.

Grace:

"It's early evening, and I'm beat. We need to go back to get some sleep before hitting the road early."

When they arrive at the motel, they fall into their beds, too exhausted for anything else, and fall asleep.

The following morning, Grace wakes up first with a jolt. The clock says 9 a.m.

Grace:

"Hey guys, time to get up. It's later than when I wanted to leave."

Quickly, they get ready and pack the VW. It's then that Grace sees the rear driver's side tire is flat. She's never changed a tire before.

Grace:

"Do either of you know how to change a flat?"

They both shake their heads.

Grace:

"Shit. What do we do now?"

The state trooper from the night before is driving by, sees them and pulls in.

"You have a problem, ma'am?"

Grace:

"Yes, officer."

State trooper:

"Maybe I can be of assistance."

He expertly changes the tire.

Grace:

"I don't know what we would have done without you."

State trooper:

"All in a day's work, ma'am."

Their trip home is uneventful and peaceful, a welcome change from the craziness of the past two days. They arrive home the night of July 3, 1976, the day before the U.S. Bicentennial Independence Day celebration. Grace and the boys start unloading the van and walk into the kitchen, where Luke's dad and Ricky are at the table, and Luke's

mom is cooking for the next day. The three are discussing

plans for the following day.

Luke's mom:

"Aren't you three a sight for sore eyes."

Grace:

"We had a lot of fun."

Luke's mom:

"I'm glad you're all home safely. How did the boys do?"

Grace:

"No problem at all, Mom."

Luke and Mark look at each other and laugh, thinking about

the trip.

Luke's dad:

"Ricky, why don't you help them finish unloading."

Ricky:

"Can't they do it themselves? It wasn't my trip."

Luke's dad:

"Just help. We all need to get up early for the setup at the

high school."

Ricky begrudgingly goes out to the VW with Mark and

Luke, and they finish unloading.

Grace:

"Mom, I'm gonna take off."

Luke's mom:

"Just stay. I need your help getting ready in the morning."

Grace:

"Okay."

Grace goes to the hallway closet and gets out sheets and a blanket for sleeping on the living room sofa.

Luke's mom:

"Good night, honey."

Luke and Mark are back in Luke's bedroom. Their pile of trip stuff sits on the floor by the windows. They both look at the pile and then each other.

Luke:

"How about we deal with this tomorrow?"

Mark:

"Sounds good to me."

As he falls asleep, Mark thinks about his mom, dad and sisters celebrating July 4th on Kwaj with a community picnic and watching fireworks shot over the lagoon. He

misses his family.

Chapter 9

Dawn is breaking on what looks to be a sunny and warm day, typical for summer in Santa Cruz.

Luke's mom and dad have a lot to do but linger in bed a bit longer, enjoying each other's company.

Their bedroom is on the first floor, near the front entrance.

The room's focal point is the bed, with its headboard against the side wall and nightstands on both sides. Reading material and glasses sit on Luke's mom's nightstand. A work alarm clock sits on his dad's. A wooden hope chest at the foot of the bed stores bedding and linens. As they lie in bed together, they watch the sun rise through the window, which faces the street.

Luke's mom:

"How did you sleep?"

Luke's dad:

"A bit restless. My mind is full of things for today. You?"

Luke's mom:

"Same. It's going to be a busy day for all of us. When I was reading last night, I realized it was the first time in a while that all three of our kids are sleeping at home."

Luke's dad:

"How're you holding up?"

Luke's mom:

"A bit worn out. The last few weeks have been busy. But nothing lasts forever."

Luke's dad:

"The summertime maintenance and cleaning at work is hectic."

Luke's mom:

"That's every summer."

Luke's dad:

"You're right. What's really draining me is hoping Ricky will get on with his life."

Luke's mom:

"The kids have to go at their own pace."

Luke's dad:

"I still wish something would light a fire under Ricky."

Luke's mom kisses her husband:

"Things have a way of working out. I'm getting up."

Luke's dad looks at his clock.

"It's time."

They each have a dresser across from the bed. Luke's dad puts on his janitor uniform, and his mom gets on her cooking clothes.

Luke's mom:

"Luke and Mark are getting along well."

Luke's dad:

"The visit has been good for both of them."

Luke's mom moisturizes her hands:

"What do you think about Mark coming back next summer?"

Luke's dad brushes his hair.

"Talk with Joan and Max before promising anything to the boys. I'm going to make sure they're getting up, as well as Ricky. I'm going to need lots of help with setting up."

Luke's mom:

"I'll get breakfast ready."

As Luke's mom is walking to the kitchen, she sees Grace putting away her sheets and blanket.

Grace:

"Morning, Mom."

Luke's mom:

"How did you sleep, honey?"

Grace:

"Good. I was beat from all the driving. During the long stretches on the road, I wished Luke had his license."

Luke's mom:

"Anything else you want to share about the trip?"

Grace:

"We had a few hiccups. To save money, we tried sleeping in the van the first night, but a state trooper made us move, so I found a cheap motel."

Luke's mom:

"You always should expect bumps in the road. The key is how you handle them."

Realizing some things are better left unsaid, Grace opts not to tell her mom about the late-night skinny dipping or losing the boys at Magic Mountain.

Grace:

"We had a flat yesterday morning, but that same state trooper was driving by and took pity on us."

Luke's mom:

"Will wonders ever cease?"

Grace:

"I remember how you've dealt with bumps. Like you patching holes on our jeans to make them last longer."

Luke's mom:

"I started a fad."

They laugh.

Luke's mom:

"Let's make breakfast."

As the family is finishing breakfast, Luke's dad gives directions:

"Okay, guys, be ready in five minutes."

Ricky:

"Dad, I'll meet ya there."

Luke's dad:

"Don't take too long."

Luke and Mark get ready and ride with Luke's dad to the high school, and Ricky shows up right behind them.

Luke's dad:

"Luke and Mark, you concentrate on putting up bunting on the building. Ricky, help me with the folding picnic tables and chairs and putting up a stage for speeches and Grace's band.

Luke and Mark get supplies from the storage shed, while Luke's dad and Ricky bring out the tables and chairs stored beneath the bleachers in the gym. They all work for several hours straight, and for once Ricky doesn't complain.

Later in the morning, other volunteers join in the effort, including setting up for sports competitions. This speeds up progress, and by noon, Luke's dad determines everything is ready. The group heads home to shower and change for the festivities.

By early afternoon, people start arriving, and the tables become heavy with potluck food. Kids jump inside a bouncy house, and an Uncle Sam stilt walker gives away noisemakers. Adolescent boys set off firecrackers in the parking lot. Luke spots Stephanie in the crowd and goes to meet her.

The Santa Cruz mayor welcomes everyone and reads the Declaration of Independence to the crowd. Luke and Stephanie leave the crowd and walk toward the gym.

Luke:

"Stef, I'm glad you and your folks came."

Stephanie:

"Me too."

Luke:

"How have you been?"

Stephanie:

"Fine."

Luke:

"Just fine? Are you still angry with me?"

Stephanie:

"Not as much as before. I agree with some of what you said, but I'm getting the short end of the stick when it comes to your attention."

Luke:

"Yeah, there is truth in that. But I only have so many hours in a day."

Stephanie:

"But how you spend those hours tells me your priorities, and lately I'm not one. I don't get it."

Luke:

"I told you … Mark is in Santa Cruz for a short time. When he leaves, we'll be together again."

Stephanie:

"Yeah, but you'll still have your job, and school and sports start soon."

Luke:

"You'll have classes too."

Stephanie:

"Yes, but besides studying, you're my top priority!"

Luke:

"You're important to me, but I won't make you promises I can't keep."

Stephanie:

"If I didn't know better, I'd think you're seeing someone else."

Luke:

"Come on, Stef. Don't be like this."

Stephanie:

"Like what?"

Luke:

"Clingy."

Stephanie:

"Clingy? I call this being a good girlfriend!"

Luke:

"Stef …"

Stephanie:

"I call this you not being a true boyfriend!"

Luke thinks about what to say next, but he's out of time.

Stephanie:

"You need time on your own to think about your lack of appreciation for what we have."

Luke:

"Stef, you don't mean that."

Stephanie:

"Yes, I do!"

With that, Stephanie storms out to find her parents and go home. The gym door slams behind her.

Luke sits on the bleachers and slumps forward, shaking his head. He takes deep breaths to calm down and then walks back to the soccer field.

While Luke and Stephanie are in the gym, Mark goes to Luke's mom for food at one of the serving tables.

Luke's mom:

"Do you want some of my fried chicken?"

Mark:

"Please. I'll take some corn on the cob as well."

Luke's mom:

"It's great having you here. Luke's going to miss you."

Mark:

"You think so?"

Luke's mom nods several times and smiles.

The picnic continues into the early evening, with an apple pie-eating contest that Ricky wins, a three-legged race in which Luke and his dad compete, and a giant tug-of-war. The event ends with Grace and her band performing a set of Fleetwood Mac covers. Neighbors clean up and say their goodbyes, and the Bordets head over to the beach for fireworks. After parking, they find an open spot on the beach among the other families and couples. Luke's mom and dad and Grace sit on folding beach chairs while Mark and Luke lie on a blanket. Ricky walks off to find his buddies. The fireworks crowd also uses the boardwalk benches.

As they wait for the show to begin, Luke and Mark talk softly.

Mark:

"What happened with you and Stephanie this afternoon?"

Luke:

"We had a big fight. She accused me of cheating on her and left."

Mark:

"That's tough. What's important, though, is the truth."

Luke:

"I appreciate you saying that, Mark, but I don't think it will help."

Mark:

"I'm here for you, man."

Independence Day 1976 climaxes with red and white fireworks exploding over the dark-blue Pacific.

Chapter 10

Luke and Mark are at recess from classes at Kwajalein's George Seitz Elementary School. The coral-sand playground, full of metal equipment, is hot and bright. Several of the boys' classmates swing on a row of swings, others do flips from parallel bars and some climb on a monkey bars shaped like a geodesic dome. Luke and Mark compete at tetherball, seeing who can wrap the ball all the way around the pole first.

Mr. Healy, their fifth-grade teacher, stands and watches the children. Tall and in his 50s, he has a full head of wavy white hair. He loudly blows the whistle hanging around his neck three times.

"Okay, everyone. I need you to get in two lines, one for girls and one for boys. It's time for our class picture."

The girls form their line quickly, but the boys roughhouse, and Mr. Healy blows his whistle again.

"Simmer down. Mr. Jackson only has so much time to get these pictures."

Once the boys are in order, Mr. Healy leads the group to a large tree with a horizontal branch strong enough to hold four of them. Those boys climb and sit on the branch, with Mark at one end and Luke at the other, and the rest of the children and Mr. Healy settle in beneath them. Nate Jackson, the island's official photographer, adjusts the camera settings and brings the image into focus.

Nate:

"Say 'Yokwe'."

This relaxes the class, and as they smile he snaps a series of shots, including the one published in the *Ekatak*, the school's yearbook.

As Nate is working, the sky fills with storm clouds, and a torrent of water is soon coming down. As Mark, Luke and the others on the tree are climbing off, the branch cracks loudly and gives way.

The boys lose their balance and fall. The fall feels like floating, and Luke sees himself cleaning Mark's cuts in the grocery storage room, then arguing with Stef on the Santa Cruz boardwalk as they eat lunch. Luke sees himself scaring off the mountain lion at the lake, but this time instead of running off, the lion attacks him and Mark.

With a jolt, Luke awakens from the nightmare. His skin and T-shirt are damp with sweat. As his mind reorients, Luke sees Mark's bed is made and empty, and he hears the bedroom door open.

Mark comes in wearing a T-shirt that says "Almost Heaven Kwajalein."

Mark:

"You're up."

Luke:

"Hey. Where were you?"

Mark:

"Went for one last bike ride. Rode by the high school. The cleared-off stage is the only thing left from yesterday."

Luke:

"Guess my dad decided to deal with that today."

Mark:

"Also rode around the neighborhood. It's been a great trip."

Luke:

"I agree."

Mark:

"I may even miss Ricky teasing us."

Mark packs, and after a final breakfast with Luke and his mom, the three leave for the airport. The drive is rainy, with plenty of lightning and thunder. Luke's mom concentrates on getting there safely.

At the airport, Luke's mom pulls into the short-term parking garage. Mark gets his luggage from the truck bed, pulling it from underneath the blue tarp keeping it dry. The three go into the terminal, and Mark checks his luggage at the United counter, keeping his backpack. As they go through security and to Mark's gate, the boys talk about their visit.

Luke:

"Remember the diving competition at Stef's pool?"

Mark:

"I let you win."

Luke:

"I won fair and square!"

Mark:

"Guess you'll never know for sure."

Luke:

"And what about when you threw up at the boardwalk?"

Mark:

"I'd rather forget."

At the gate, the attendant updates the passengers:

"Aloha and good morning, folks. The weather has cleared, and we'll be boarding shortly."

Luke's mom pulls Mark into a motherly embrace:

"We've enjoyed having you, Mark."

Mark:

"Thanks, Mrs. Bordet. It's been great."

Mark turns to Luke, and they hug for a long time, much different from how they greeted each other on Mark's arrival.

Mark:

"I'm going to miss our nightly talks."

Luke:

"Me too."

Mark's row is called, and he gets in line.

Luke and his mom watch as he boards. Once Mark goes into the walkway, Luke and his mom walk over to the window for a better view of Mark's plane.

Luke's mom puts her arm around her son's shoulder.

"It's been a nice visit."

They now can see Mark at his window seat and wave to him. He waves back.

The pilot backs the plane away from the gate, taxis to the runway and, after getting the air controller's okay, rapidly builds speed until the plane breaks free from the ground and ascends into the overcast sky. As the plane climbs, Mark watches until San Francisco is lost in the clouds.

Mark has the row to himself. He reflects on his stay, thinking about being more independent away from his family, whom he looks forward to seeing. The plane starts to bounce as it hits a pocket of turbulence.

The captain comes on the PA system.

"Folks, make sure your seat belts are securely fastened. We're not fully clear yet from the Bay Area's bad weather."

Mark checks his seat belt and assures himself the bumpiness will pass. But the plane takes an unexpected 2,000-foot dive. Overhead bins pop open, and carry-on luggage falls onto passengers and into the aisles. Adults scream and children cry.

The pilot comes back on, his voice urgent.

"Everyone needs to brace for an ocean landing. God help us."

The passengers assume the crash position, leaning forward and holding their hands over their heads.

Mark realizes he will never see his family again and starts crying. As the plane is about to smash into the water, he passes out.

Chapter 11

Carlos sits in a private hospital room in the Neurology and Neurosurgery Unit of Cedars-Sinai Medical Center in Los Angeles. It's 10 p.m., and the window behind him reveals a brightly lit Los Angeles skyline.

At 59 years old, five-and-a-half feet tall and 145 pounds, Carlos is half Japanese, half Latino and was adopted as a baby by a family in Peru, where he lived until moving to the United States in his late 20s. He is watching a telenovela on the TV.

Asleep in the bed next to Carlos is 57-year-old Mark, a dead ringer for Stanley Tucci. He has a several-day growth of black and gray stubble. A wrapping of gauze bandages covers the top of his head.

The TV begins to waken Mark, who opens his eyes and breathes deeply. He looks around the room, at the monitors on his right and then at Carlos.

Carlos:

"Hey, you."

Mark:

"Hey."

Carlos:

"How are you feeling?"

Mark:

"Out of it."

A nurse by training, Carlos puts his hand on Mark's forehead and glances at the monitors.

Carlos:

"I'll be right back."

Mark is disoriented, puts his hand on his head and wonders why it's covered in bandages.

Rhea, the floor nurse, comes into the room with Carlos. She pulls out a penlight and examines Mark's eyes.

Rhea:

"How are you feeling?"

Mark:

"My head's pounding, and my arms and legs are sore."

Rhea:

"Just relax."

Mark:

"I can't focus."

Rhea takes out a prefilled syringe of medicine and injects it into the fluid bag hanging next to the bed. She briefly talks on her cellphone.

Rhea:

"The doctor will be in shortly."

She reads Mark's monitors and makes notes on his chart. His agitation subsides as the medicine takes effect.

Carlos:

"Buddy, you're doing good."

Mark smiles weakly at Carlos.

Head-injury specialist Dr. Jeffrey Cohn comes into the room. In his early 50s with a receding hairline, Dr. Cohn looks at Mark's chart.

Dr. Cohn:

"How are you feeling, Mr. Sahl?"

Mark:

"Like a Mack truck hit me."

Dr. Cohn:

"You've been in a coma for the past three days."

Mark has trouble registering this information.

 "What?"

Dr. Cohn:

"You hit your head badly after falling off your bike and got knocked out. After the accident, they couldn't wake you and medevacked you here. We've been hoping you'd come out of it."

Mark looks questioningly at Carlos.

Carlos:

"We came to California for a five-day fundraiser bike ride you were doing with your high school friend, Luke."

Things start to register for Mark.

Dr. Cohn:

"It's great you are awake. It's best you rest, but stay awake."

Rhea:

"Carlos, you know where to find me."

Dr. Cohn and Rhea leave.

Mark:

"I've really been out for three days?"

Carlos nods.

"But you're back."

Mark:

"I'm starting to remember. Luke and I had reconnected earlier this year for the first time since I moved to Florida."

Carlos:

"He emailed you about the fundraiser."

Mark:

"And I reached out to him to see how he was doing, and we started corresponding again."

Carlos:

"Early on, you got excited about the idea of doing the ride with Luke."

Mark:

"You encouraged me to wait to discuss the idea with him. After a month of emailing back and forth, I asked."

Carlos:

"And he said yes."

Mark:

"I remember my training rides."

Carlos:

"You got pretty obsessed."

Mark:

"And how you pranked me when I asked you to come with!"

Carlos:

"Yeah, a song and dance about a nursing class I had to do the week of the ride."

Realizing Mark is getting too excited, Carlos suggests they watch TV and finds a music concert.

Carlos:

"I'll be back in a few."

Carlos squeezes Mark's hand. Mark's smile is stronger.

Carlos goes to the waiting room down the hall and calls Mark's sister Lisa, a doctor in Hawaii.

Carlos:

"Hi Lisa. He's awake."

Lisa:

"That's great."

Carlos:

"His neurologist agrees. He's having Mark stay awake, so we're watching TV. I'll call you later."

As Carlos approaches the room, he hears Mark singing along with the concert. Carlos watches Mark from the hall until the song ends.

Mark:

"My lovely tenor."

Carlos:

"I like your singing."

They watch until the end. Rhea returns.

Rhea:

"How're you feeling?"

Mark:

"Headache's gone. My thoughts are clearer."

Rhea:

"We're going to have you try sleeping for the night. I'll come in every few hours."

Carlos turns off the TV and kisses Mark, Rhea dims the lights, and they leave. Mark quickly drifts off. In the waiting room, Carlos calls Lisa back.

Lisa:

"Mom's with me."

Joan:

"Hi, Carlos."

Carlos:

"Joan, he's doing well."

Joan:

"Thank God."

Carlos:

"He's starting to remember things, but groggy."

Lisa:

"The cobwebs still need to clear."

Carlos:

"He was awake for two hours, until his doctor said it was okay to sleep for the night."

Lisa:

"I'm going to call Dr. Cohn in the morning."

Joan:

"When is our flight?"

Lisa:

"We take off from Lihue tomorrow at 10 a.m."

Carlos:

"When will you get here?"

Lisa:

"We should be at the hospital by 9 p.m. Michele wants to video chat with Mark since she can't come in from Kwaj."

Lisa:

"You must be wiped out."

Carlos:

"I'm grateful he woke up."

Joan:

"Us too."

After Joan and Lisa hang up, Carlos calls Luke and Steve, who will visit in the morning. Carlos goes back to his chair next to Mark, who is asleep. He tips back the padded recliner and settles in with a pillow and blanket. Carlos sleeps through Rhea's first several checks on Mark but wakes up the last time.

Rhea:

"Sorry to wake you."

Carlos:

"Two of Mark's friends will be here later this morning, and his mom and sister are arriving in the evening."

Rhea:

"We'll keep the visits brief. It should be fine."

When dawn breaks, Mark is already awake as Carlos opens his eyes.

Mark:

"Buenas dias, Carlos."

Carlos:

"Buenas dias. ¿Como estas?

Mark:

"Muy bien. ¿Y tu?"

Carlos:

"It's good to hear your gringo accent."

Mark laughs:

"How did you sleep?"

Carlos:

"I was in the chair, so not the best."

Mark:

"Didn't you get a hotel room?"

Carlos:

"Yes. I go back for naps but wanted to stay with you for the night."

Mark:

"How did I fall off the bike?"

Carlos:

"In San Luis Obispo, you and Luke were rounding a curve in the rain, and you lost control. You fell down the road's embankment and hit your head on a tree trunk."

Mark:

"Ouch."

Carlos:

"It knocked you out. Your helmet softened the blow. The medic for the event examined you. When he couldn't wake you up, he called for help."

Mark:

"Where were you?"

Carlos:

"You remember Steve and I were driving down the coast, following you and Luke?"

Mark:

"Yes."

Carlos:

"We were on a walking tour in San Luis Obispo. Luke told us you were flown to L.A., so we drove straight here."

Mark:

"Where are Luke and Steve?"

Carlos:

"Luke decided to finish the race after they told him there wasn't anything he could do until you woke up. Steve stayed with me the first day in L.A., then he went back to Santa Monica."

Mark:

"I'm glad he was with you."

Carlos:

"They're stopping by later this morning."

Rhea comes back carrying a tray with water, applesauce and Jell-O.

Rhea:

"Take some sips of water."

At first, Mark takes small sips. After Rhea gives him a thumbs up, he swallows fully.

Mark:

"Didn't realize water could taste so good."

Rhea:

"Go ahead and eat the Jell-O."

Mark has no adverse response, so Rhea has him eat the applesauce as well.

Rhea:

"That's enough eating for now. Continue with the water as you need it. We'll try solid food later."

Mark:

"I'm hungry."

Rhea:

"That's a good sign, but we need to ease you into it."

Rhea leaves with the tray.

Carlos:

"I'm going to step out for a little."

Carlos takes his toiletry bag with him from the wide windowsill. Mark looks out the window. It's sunny in downtown Los Angeles. There's no smog, so he sees the mountains off in the distance. Mark closes his eyes and doses on and off until Carlos comes back. They watch the local news.

Later, Luke and Steve arrive with a knock on the open door.

Luke:

"Hey, Mark!"

Mark:

"Hi, Luke. Sorry to put a damper on the ride."

Luke:

"Don't even think about that."

Steve:

"We're glad you're getting better."

Luke:

"How are you feeling?"

Mark:

"I was out of it last night. Today's better."

Mark turns his attention to Steve:

"Carlos reminded me you two drove down the coast together."

Luke's partner:

"We enjoyed time with you and Luke in the evenings and had a blast in the van during the days, cranking up ABBA and the Bee Gees, and stopping along the way to take in the scenery."

Carlos:

"When you found out I had never been to San Francisco, you took me to Golden Gate Park, the Presidio and the Castro District before we headed down the coast."

Mark:

"Our dinner the night before the ride was fun — you guys surprised me with a birthday cake."

Luke:

"We had to celebrate."

Mark:

"How did the rest of the ride go?"

Luke:

"It went well but wasn't quite the same without you three."

Mark:

"I was there in my dreams. Speaking of which, I had a doozie while I was out for the past three days."

Luke:

"About what?"

Mark:

"My first visit with you and your family in Santa Cruz."

Luke:

"Wow."

Mark:

"I know it's cliché, but I feel like Dorothy waking up at the end of the *Wizard of Oz*."

Carlos:

"Now you're going too far. Remember, I'm the melodramatic one."

Mark:

"Ha ha ha. But my story didn't begin in black and white —

it went right to Technicolor."

Carlos:

"Okay, Dorothy."

Mark:

"Maybe I had it because of the emails Luke and I

exchanged when I was living in Puerto Rico. We talked

about growing up, and Luke had surmised we got along

well right from the start because we're both gay, even

though we didn't really know it at the time."

Luke points at Mark's bandaged head.

"Could've just been from that nasty gash to your noggin."

Mark:

"Whatever it was, it didn't feel like a dream. I thought I was reliving that first summer in Santa Cruz."

Carlos:

"You should write a book about it."

Mark:

"I've always wanted to do that."

Carlos:

"A perfect opportunity. Your doctor said you have to take it easy for a while after we get back to Florida. With your bipolar disorder, you'll need something to occupy your brain during recovery."

Mark:

"I'm not sure. I'll have to sleep on it."

The three look at Mark as his expression goes from serious to smiling, and they all start laughing.

He is on his way to a full recovery.

www.ingramcontent.com/pod-product-compliance
Lightning Source LLC
Chambersburg PA
CBHW041749310726
48978CB00011BB/371